ALSO BY ARI NEWMAN

AMERICA FIRST A Modern Fable

The Mueller Report Uncertainty

Mrs. Vanderbilt

Primogeniture

VOLUME I

Ari Newman

Mrs. Vanderbilt

To Mom and Dad,
I love you so much

Mrs. Vanderbilt

This is a work of fiction. Names, characters, places, and incidents are either the product of the author's imagination or are used fictitiously, and any resemblances to actual persons, living or dead, business establishments, events, or locales is entirely coincidental

MRS. VANDERBILT

Mrs. Vanderbilt Novel LLC published by arrangement with the author

All rights reserved
Hard Cover Copyright © 2022 Ari Newman
Copyright © 2018 Ari Newman
Edited by Dianne Z. Newman
A derivative work of THE HOUSE OF VANDERBILT
© 2008 Ari Newman
Copyright Registration Number: Pau 3-355-100

This book, or parts thereof, may not be reproduced in any form without permission from Mrs. Vanderbilt Novel LLC and Ari Newman except in the case of brief quotations embodied in critical articles and reviews.

The Library of Congress has catalogued the U.S. edition as follows:
Copyright Registration Number: Pau003486976
ISBN: 13:978-0-9986672-3-2
Hard Cover ISBN: 9798365295728

First Edition Published 2018
WRITTEN IN JERUSALEM ISRAEL
PUBLISHED IN THE UNITES STATES OF AMERICA

Acknowledgements

THIS WORK WAS ORIGINALLY based upon a manuscript for a TV series, converted for a TV movie, re-written again as a theatrical film and is now being released as a three volume book series.

This is an alternate historical work of fiction, however many publications were used for research including these wonderful books:

Consuelo and Alva Vanderbilt by Amanda Mackenzie Stuart
Fortune's Children by Arthur T. Vanderbilt II
The First Tycoon by T.J. Stiles
The Vanderbilt Women by Clarice Stasz
The Vanderbilts by Jerry E. Patterson
When the Astors Owned New York by Justin Kaplan

Although not affiliated with this project the publisher and author want to encourage its readers and other interested parties to visit the Newport Mansions which are owned and operated through the great work of the non-profit Preservation Society of Newport County. www.newportmansions.org

The Biltmore in Asheville, NC is also a wonderful place for a vacation and an opportunity to learn more about the Vanderbilt family.

Mrs. Vanderbilt

Contents

Acknowledgements 2
Dedication 6
Prologue 8
A Royal Wedding 12
The Akedah 25
The Commodore 41
The Court of Newport 79
Epilogue 140
Dramatis Personae 141

Mrs. Vanderbilt

Dedication

A WONDERFUL SMILE COMES ACROSS my face that will not fade when I think about all the people over the years who were a part of my life; most importantly the teachers from my very beginning.

We can all be students and teachers.

Dedicated in honor of my parents
Dr. Martin & Dianne Z. Newman
&
Erica, Josh, Hannah, and Jonah
& good friend Josh Blumenthal

In memory of those loved who were lost too soon:
Jeremy Blumenthal
Marc Dwares
Deborah Feldstein
Jennifer Miller
Joshua Rubin

BOSTON STRONG

Mrs. Vanderbilt

Prologue

THE WINDS OF WAR are once again blowing in Europe and I present this work now pursuant to the stipulations and recommendations of the wills and manuscripts of those involved in this story and most importantly with the permission and encouragement of artist and philanthropist Gertrude Vanderbilt Whitney.

European Manifest Destiney is now a Nazi mandate and neither Neville Chamberlin, Theodore Roosevelt, or Joseph Stalin can prevent it, limit its expansion or defeat it unless the powers that be find the courage to recognize foreign policy initiatives that have failed and quickly reverse course in the four corners of the earth: Asia, Arabia, North Africa and the struggle between the fascist, the communist, and the populist in Europe.

This once reporter for the New York Daily Herald does not attempt to draw conclusions or express a preference with the material within covered. Rather, holding my lawyer pen I have endeavored to piece together a complex narrative combining personal journals and essays, irrefutable facts, an autobiography and a fictional manuscript which was originally penned by someone unknown, but which I have long believed to be the hand of Mrs. Vanderbilt.

What do you think?

Respectfully submitted in the spirit of peace and prosperity for all peoples everywhere; and

Dedicated to the memory of man's best friend throughout the world and who have journeyed with me on all the adventures, expeditions, and travels, through good times and bad, and who will always be remembered as my family: Kelev (the Hebrew word for dog), Malka (the Hebrew word for Queen), Kelev II, Trooper, Nikko, Brady, and Carlos.

J. Rambler Perkins
Jerusalem, 1938

In 1877, when Commodore Cornelius Vanderbilt died, his estate was worth was one hundred million dollars. Since 1525 no one man had accumulated such wealth. Today he would be worth over $167 billion dollars.

The First Plutocrat

Mrs. Vanderbilt

A Royal Wedding

Looking in from the outside
you will never understand.
Looking out from the inside
I can never explain.

SO GLORIOUS WAS THE STAGE set for those who dream of aristocratic privilege that even the heirs of New York City's highest society stood in awe, waving their hands as one corner after the next swelled with crowds standing in the November morning sun. Fifth Avenue was finally as famous as the Champs–Élysées though it would never be the same. "Extra, Extra, read all about it. British Duke to marry American heiress!"

Status Quo Ante Bellum evolved from a political position in the early 19th century ending the War of 1812 with Britain to the need for our two countries' social status to be reciprocally respected as our national borders. During the ensuing generations, including a scientific evolution followed by an industrial revolution, the pursuit was not to rule in military power or in intellect but rather in riches, by way of who could generate the largest fortune, who could spend the most extravagantly, and who could gild the most lavishly. Seeming to possess wealth was far more important than actually having any. Working for one's money was the new American tradition, while inheritance was the European model. Of course only a few lived this life, but to us who didn't know any other way and certainly weren't acquainted with anyone like you, Victoria, which is why our friendship was so unique and special. Although the bride's father knew the most important social event and political spectacle taking place in the city was a farce, we did not, nor did the British Duke and his American bride.

St. Thomas Episcopalian Church was the center of the chaos, surrounded by the castles of the richest families in America and perhaps, the world. So great was this day in 1895 that endless numbers of the ladies from the best families had been up all night with their servants preparing their best gowns, styling their hair to perfection, and choosing just the right shoes -- and not one of them had been invited! Though usually filled with horse drawn carriages with footmen and Royal House Guards who would parade American royalty past the palaces that adorned this exclusive avenue, today the streets were empty of traffic. As far as the eye could see, these normally demure ladies were graceless as they pushed and shoved their way past the bastion of policemen. Four thousand invitations had been dispatched around the world and it took hours for the invited guests to navigate the hedge maze of onlookers, newspaper reporters, and photographers. Once through the barricades, guests passed footmen from the most-noble houses still waiting for their charges to arrive. The last layer of defense were the Pinkertons. Armed and ready, they were accustomed to dealing with the new generation of striking workers, but on this occasion they were the private muscle on hand to assist the police in avoiding violence.

"Sergeant Grimes, I have ordered Captain Donnelly's men not to use clubs on these women. Your men shall follow the same order", instructed Inspector Cartwright, an aggressive forty-year old in charge of the wedding's security. On most days, Cartwright directed the elite officers who were responsible for guarding the American royal houses. Should extreme circumstances necessitate beatings, extortion, cover ups, corporate espionage…such was implemented in private or, if an example was necessary, in public. When required to stand before a judicial court he was there to demand, not to petition. Among the households he was the Colonel of the House Guards. His men were of military descent, highly educated, and from the upwardly mobile families who dreamed of being invited to the wedding. It was no small thing for one's son to be standing post under Cartwright – something about which a father would freely boast.

"Inspector, we do not have enough men to hold back these crowds. It is only ten thirty and the wedding is not till noon."

"I repeat, clubs shall not be used. Imagine if by accident a mistress is injured by a nightstick or pushed into the path of a horse. Maintain order. Stand fast men."

America had rarely, if ever, experienced something so titanic! Royal burials and coronations in London and Paris and in the Italian States would bring together Europe's princes and prime ministers, oriental Emperors, Arabian sheiks and African kings, and heads of state and governors from across the oceans to the South American colonies and lands and islands far beyond.

The eyes of the world and the ears of the press were following every detail of this day. Since the summer when the Duke first arrived in America to claim his bride, New York society had but one focus. If successful, European nobles would be eager to marry into new American prosperity, while the American matriarchs were just as eager for their children to attain European title and status.

St. Thomas' Church sparkled with the pomp and splendor of the costumes and regalia, mixing French and English textures from its post Gothic limestone exterior to its flamboyant sandstone interior. Inside, the guests were fighting for seats as ushers shuffled the newest arrivals based on status, in a waltz of musical chairs. The pews in the front were intended for the peerages from New York, Washington, Philadelphia, and Boston along with American politicians and European nobles. As the Carnegies, Rockefellers, and Morgans were ushered to their seats, other guests stood on their chairs to catch a glimpse.

If the fairy tale outside could satisfy an appetite, inside was the dream of every little girl to be a princess forever. The cupola rose to the heavens. Draped along the walls from the ceiling to the floor were garlands of greens and laurels intertwined with lilies and roses. It was as if the colors of the rainbow were infused with the scents of the morning dew. The columns were covered with pink and white chrysanthemums, ropes of white baby's breath, and in the center stood torches covered with pink and white roses.

Noon was approaching and America was about to have its first official European duchess. A side door opened and walking to the alter was the Bishop of New York, Bishop Potter, and the Chaplain at the Duke's Blenheim Palace, Reverend Burnett – followed by a stream of other Bishops, Ministers and Rectors. Behind the clergy, an orchestra played Beethoven, Mozart, Lemmens, Wagner, and Tchaikovsky. At the very front of the church the "grandfather" of the American banking industry, JP Morgan, greeted his best customers and loyal friends, though it was the head of the Vanderbilt empire that he was most courting.

"It certainly is a mob scene out there", Morgan commented to sixty-two year old attorney Chauncey Depew. Although not a Vanderbilt by blood, Chauncey was President of the New York Central Railroad Company and had served the family since its founding patriarch, Cornelius Vanderbilt, transformed his steamship business into the world's largest railroad enterprise.

Seizing the opportunity, Morgan and Chauncey were quickly interrupted by the ebullient socialite, Ward McAllister, "Well what would you expect? What's important is that we are all here and that the wedding is on. Let the party begin!"

"I'm so surprised you were able to convince all three ladies to attend", responded Chauncey.

"Just required a bit of finesse, and shall we say, compromise, mixed with a dash of persuasion. As Mr. Morgan calls it, some 'persuasive negotiation'. If we are honest, my dear Chauncey, who marries who is far less important than negotiating which dress made by which designer would each lady wear. Public perception is the Lord of Lords. As my sweet mother would always remind me, 'in order to feel good, you must look good'."

"Mr. McAllister, I trust this "compromise" did not involve any business arrangements? You haven't undone any deals or renegotiated anything, have you?" asked Morgan.

"Why Mr. Morgan, I would never have attempted to undermine you; maybe to be under you, but not to undermine you," McAllister joked. "No, I just simply suggested that since the families are intertwined in business and society that they enter the nave together so as not to disrupt the proper order of society. Not one of them wanted to be the lady who refused, for that would have had a negative effect on one's standing."

Morgan has the last word, aimed at McAllister, "you're doing the Lord's work."

The roars and the cheers reverberated from the street into the church where the rear doors of the sanctuary opened, and every single guest quickly turned to the back so as not to miss a moment. Those along the wall stood on their chairs, struggling to stay upright so as not to fall like dominos. Two ushers entered, followed by Mrs. Vanderbilt, Mrs. Astor, and

Alva Vanderbilt escorted by footmen from each household dressed in either red Vanderbilt livery or blue Astor livery. The footmen were all the same height, dressed in formal fancy coat, knee breeches, silk stockings, and powdered hair wigs. The women wore gowns made of silk with matching hats that were designed to compete with each other.

Just as the trio arrived at the front of the church an uproar was heard from the outside onlookers as the rear doors were opened again by two ushers. Entering were the bridesmaids and some of the most famous princesses in America: Belle Wilson, her sister May Wilson Goelet, Carrie Astor, and Esther Hunt. As the bridesmaids made their way to the altar, they were joined by the groomsmen who wore frock coats, striped trousers and top hats.

The stage was set and the actors were all in their initial places. Negotiations had concluded and the dowry was agreed upon. Dressed in a dark grey double-breasted waistcoat with a white boutonniere and light grey gloves, the Duke entered from a side door and took his place at the altar. For the first time all morning, the outside and inside of the church were silent, awaiting the arrival of the bride. What would she be wearing? How beautiful was she going to be? Excitement filled the air as thousands of America's highborn turned their heads, staring at the closed doors at the rear of the sanctuary. The choreography had been rehearsed and as soon as the two ushers opened the doors, the conductor would wave his baton for the bridal chorus from Wagner's *Lohengrin*. The Duke glanced down at his watch. It was five minutes after twelve – the bride must be fashionably late.

The silence continued -- the minutes were ticking by. Oh how we felt for her, how you wanted to be her. You don't know what the position of an heiress is. You can't imagine. Of course worldly goods surround her. She wishes a dress, a jewel, a horse – she has it, but all the money in the world cannot bring a loving heart or a true friend. And so she sits on her throne, with her bags of money, and society bows to her because her pedestal is solid and firm and she doesn't seem quite human.

A moment passed, then another. The ushers did not move – the doors were not opening. Minutes were going by, one by one, in an apparent race between the bride arriving or running. A minute went by then another; still the doors did not open. Except for several coughs echoing round and a sneeze or two, there was dead silence. Mrs. Astor, Mrs. Vanderbilt, and Alva Vanderbilt turned from looking at the doors to looking at each other. Another minute passed and people started fidgeting in their seats. The three women sat still, displaying no emotions. What must they be thinking? How did this all happen?

Perhaps my Mama, Alice Vanderbilt, the Mrs. Vanderbilt, dreamt of me dressed in my wedding dress standing on the lawn of our Newport estate. A photographer takes my pictures with the crystal blue water cascading below the cliffs behind me. Looking back across the beautiful lawns and palatial gardens the sun sets itself behind our grand Italian summer palace guarded by footmen in Vanderbilt red court livery. Did my mother see herself looking down from the second floor veranda, smiling at my elation – a euphoric love

I thought I would never enjoy but finally unearthed? Together she and Papa see that I am finally going to be happy.

My father was Cornelius Vanderbilt II. He had inherited the Vanderbilt fortune and was the grandson and namesake to Cornelius Vanderbilt – the "Commodore" as he was known. He was my great-grandfather and the founder of the Vanderbilt railroad empire who became wealthier than all the kings and queens of Europe. Just as the lords and dukes established manor houses in Europe, here in America the Commodore had established the House of Vanderbilt. In his Royal Court he sat on the throne and viewed the American government the same way the nobles of Europe faced their houses of Parliament, in that the affairs of state would be managed by a quasi-elected body of government as the natural continuation of the principles outlined in the *Magna Carta Libertatum*. Without the perception of governance, capitalism was exclusively the domain of the business tycoons who held power and whose Houses and Royal Courts shaped American society. Now the House of Vanderbilt was ruled by my mother, Alice Vanderbilt, Queen of the Castle. She was known and admired throughout society as "Mrs. Vanderbilt."

Across the cove from our Newport estate and a short stroll down the famous Cliff Walk, a path that separates the Newport mansions from the Atlantic Ocean one hundred feet below, was a smaller villa, the Astor Beechwood mansion watched over by its footmen in the Astor blue court livery. The House of Astor was headed by its matriarch, Caroline

Astor. Society called her "Mrs. Astor" and she was revered as the Queen of Society. What did Mrs. Astor contemplate as she sat in the church waiting?

A smile crossed Mrs. Astor's face as she remembered her societal pupil, twenty-eight year old Grace Wilson, in her wedding dress curtsying before her. If Mrs. Astor was the Queen of the House of Astor, her son, John Jacob Astor IV, the Prince, and her daughter Carrie the Princess, then Grace Wilson would be the Duchess, since it was her brother who had married Princess Carrie. Was Mrs. Astor seeing her protégé in her wedding gown?

Still further past the cove along the Cliff Walk was the much larger and more luxurious estate, Alva Vanderbilt's glorious Marble House, surrounded by Vanderbilt footmen in their red court livery. Alva Vanderbilt was also a "Mrs. Vanderbilt" although no one called her that. She had married and since divorced my father's younger brother, the dashingly handsome William Kissam Vanderbilt. To her frustration in high society she was simply known as Alva. Competitiveness flowed through Alva's veins faster than falling rain and her daughter Consuelo was her pawn. If this eighteen year old heiress could properly marry, Alva's dream of victory in society could be sealed for eternity. Was Alva seeing Consuelo in her wedding gown as she sat and waited?

Compared to European palaces that were constructed over centuries, the American castles were much smaller, used as private residences, and never intended to serve as the seat of government or reflect national power. Inside, a Newport estate could rival Versailles or Buckingham Palace for its grandeur. Outside, the European palaces were not very practical, each its own city centered around its monarch. Newport itself had become a de facto palace, a fortified peninsula like an Irish castle where, inside the moat, the people in the smaller houses served the people in the bigger houses. Newport provided the nobility a haven for royal rituals whose authenticity could have been questioned and whose bureaucratic jurisdiction could have been rebelled against. Newport provided a fortress far away from the public displays of wealth in the cities which many aristocrats feared could be considered excessive and suggestive of a feudal society that would be unsustainable, especially in the eyes of the emerging middle class.

The upper echelons were afraid and needed to make sure those in the middle became afraid of those at the bottom. For the first time in America, accumulating wealth had become important to more and more people as intellect, education, and wisdom rivalled peerage. Although misunderstood, the great fear was not that those below wanted to rise, but that they sought, believing such a principle to be equitable, to bring down those above them, amounting to the destruction of the elites. The theory was simple: if the nobles ceded the center to the masses, the American monarchy would lose its tactical positioning, wealth and power. Thus, a strategy to rebuff the socialist was needed and it required that the middle classes embrace the capitalist rather than the progressive. Of course the unintended consequence had been that pesky cousin, the plutocracy.

The leaders of this feared movement, perceived as the unpatriotic enemy, would be the younger generation – as it historically is when a society advances in innovation, culture, expression, and science. In the past, those with power and influence were the wealthy and politically well-placed, almost exclusively elderly, entirely white and male, and aghast at change. However, the industrial revolution would enable the new generation to gain riches which could be used to gain power or to buy it, turning their fantasy, and the royal's nightmare of an emerging middle class, into reality.

Newport and the estates that comprised its royal compound stood at a precipice. If the pendulum were to continue swaying toward the American royals, they had to be admired. Although respect existed or was forced in the factories, the admiration of the aristocracy fell within the purview of its Queens, Princesses, Duchesses, and Ladies, just as it was in Europe. Nobody wanted a Marie Antoinette affair and therefore, although most in New York couldn't even afford to eat cake, this wedding enchanted all the little girls and their mothers, encouraging them to believe once again in their own Cinderella fairy tale, or what would later be termed, "the America Dream."

In the church, low whispers were heard. Ward McAllister motioned to the conductor to start playing something – anything. As the music started up again, the silence was broken, and the whispering in the church quickly turned into loud chatter with no one any longer focused on the rear doors. The clergy spoke with one another, while Mrs. Astor, Mrs. Vanderbilt, and Alva moved to the side of the church and spoke amongst themselves. Chauncey and Ward McAllister quickly joined them.

Chauncey told the others, "She's not coming!"

The Akedah

A woman who marries only for money
is lost like a man who marries only for beauty
and so we all must ask for forgiveness

A great blizzard had swarmed up from the Carolinas colliding with the Midwest storms that were inching their way east resulting in a catastrophic Nor'easter when the arctic winds from Canada followed a southern route alongside the Hudson River directly into New York City. Not since before the Civil War had there been such a great amount of snow. The winds whisked from one street to another, up one river and down the other, creating small tenement-sized sleeting tornadoes.

For 365 days a year, American mythology divided society into those fortunate enough to live above and those cursed to live below. During the winter months the inescapable vividness was blinding the abandonment long ago to a life of survival like a mouse escaping the prowl of the cat, by the morning sun limitless children of the city would meet their maker. There was nothing anyone could have done even if the commonality expressed an interest or bothered to notice or care. Humanity was preoccupied with materialism, capitalism, and shoes – for that matter any material item. We were blinded by them; ones worn and the one's we didn't want to see for if we had we wouldn't have seen anything except the bare feet of the children. Observed through a jaundiced eye our shoes of diamonds exploded in colors and weaved in patterns had caused many to believe in the fairy tale – even if only for a moment. Why? We don't know, but when we explored American mythology we found in the graved gutters of this frozen infamous city rodents peeking out to witness extreme selfishness. Upstairs we had survived, and in fact partied, all of those shoeless nights, and weeks, and months, and even years, while downstairs they were torn and muddy or bare and dead.

The city hadn't been this buried since before the Civil War, so in the early morning of January 1892, when a hustle and bustle surrounded the 5th Avenue home of Mrs. Vanderbilt, word quickly spread that Extra morning editions of the newspapers were going to blanket the city along with two feet of thick heavy snow.

You were there escorting Consuelo, and entered a drawing room where the Vanderbilt children had congregated, led by eleven year old Reggie trying to impress his siblings, rambling on about Grace. Neily was thinking about Grace. My friend from across the street, Harry Payne Whitney, expressed his reasons for never socializing with her. I couldn't believe I was even talking about her. I remember so vividly when you stood by and listened to this ridiculous conversation about Grace once again. I approached you and asked about your thoughts of Grace.

"She uses men and lies about it. She is obsessed with her looks although I think she will fatten up. She is without empathy. She will not give unless forced to. She is adored and worshipped, but only because she demands it. Not unlike your great friend who plays tennis down the street at the club."

These were the first words you ever spoke to me. I recall your explanation years later that you were not allowed to speak to me unless I addressed you first, and you felt certain that I would never ask such a question again, ever. It was the first of hundreds of times I would ask you that question.

The conversation finally ended in the late night as each child fell asleep in order of age, beginning with little Gladys. We all tried, but couldn't stay awake to hear Papa's news from Yale.

King Cornelius Vanderbilt sat pensively alone in his private car as his train raced from New York into Connecticut, crossing one bridge after the next. The noise echoed through Long Island Sound, reverberating back and forth above the waves. Adrift in thoughts, this commonly subtle man shifted in and out of disbelief. His consciousness hidden in his weary eyes could have been reprieving below the Manhattan streets to the lore of the forgotten children, yet he was secluded in a golden car of stately power. Focusing on the warm pleasant moments of his own childhood to counterbalance the inevitable reality in which he would soon find himself, his repeated attempts to focus on those happy memories eventually became a losing exercise. He grasped two certainties. First, his eldest son, William Henry Vanderbilt, the heir apparent to the Vanderbilt empire, was murdered less than eight hours ago at Yale University in New Haven, Connecticut. Second, until the end of time, the world could not discover the truth. Already in the next car, Chauncey Depew, the authority on all personal and confidential matters, was quickly creating an alternative narrative.

The blue Atlantic waves were crashing into the Vanderbilt train as it crossed over one bridge after the next, steaming its way past Bridgeport and into the polar city of New Haven. Though surrounded by industry along the coast, without Yale University adding luster to its grey appearance and dreary life it would have been solely an Old Haven. Poverty crossbred with the heirs to the intellectual and industrial elites guaranteeing that equitable progress would tip toe if not limp into the next century. The Negro had found shelter in the city kneading with the poor immigrants from southern Italy who were anxious to mark their identity. The city was germinating like a plant. Yale was the cultural hub surrounded by a never ending pool of workers who could populate the factories that provided the parents of the Yale students back in New York, Philadelphia, and Boston with more and more young millionaires.

Within the university was a small yet incestuously conceived masked institution; the *Skull & Bones*. Its internal existence was not known to anyone outside of its membership, and even many within did not know the other members. Gentility had also bloomed at Harvard, Cornell and

Brown. Some academically leaning others socially, like the mansions lining Prospect Avenue serving Princeton's *eating clubs*, but the *Skull & Bones* was unique. Its rights of passage consisted of secrets that were rumored throughout the city. Actions so secret, harmful, and destructive they would stand for the next thousand years. In the early nineteenth century the founders asked themselves three pivotal questions: one, what are we about and what is our purpose; two, how to keep our secret – answer, in order to do so, powerful leverage must prevail, and three, what were the ramifications, when trust was violated? The latter was viewed as the most important for it often required actions that surpassed the remedies of biblical sins. Its mask was Yale itself – the society was only open to those candidates whose ascendancy would flow like blood through the members sustaining life and privilege all of which would create the greatest secret in America; a secret that if revealed, could destroy America and the global economy. A secret so preposterous that the few who speculated on the existence of something similar, but far less nefarious, would be viewed as lunacy thinking. A secret that for those who even approached the periphery to the truth could simply vanish into the abysm.

    The Vanderbilt train arrived at the New Haven depot, where a crowd of several hundred had gathered. Cornelius Vanderbilt understood the reality, and quickly transitioned from burial and mourning to future coronation, as succession was his primary concern. Chauncey knocked on the door and before he received a "come in", he was already sitting before King Cornelius who asked, "What will they find?"

"Well, what do you want them to?"

"The Inspector will inform the newspapers that he died of typhoid fever?"

"That's correct, sir."

The official cause of his son's death had been decided long ago, and would be maintained as long as the Vanderbilts could exert such control. King Cornelius rose and slightly slid the curtain to glance at the crowd gathered. To comfort his sovereign, Chauncey offered, "Many of them are your workers. They are here to support you."

"Chauncey, how did he actually? Do we know yet?"

"Inspector Cartwright has two of his best men assigned."

In the editorial offices of the "New York Daily Herald", Edna Milli and JR Perkins were in heated debate. They were finally together as Perkins had been up all night trying to get a confirmation of William's death, while Edna and four to five hundred other journalists had gathered at the Vanderbilt Fifth Avenue palace.

The Daily Herald was about to print that Cornelius' son had been found dead and many people would be fired if Perkins' source was inaccurate. He needed further confirmation.

At heart Edna Milli was an investigative journalist at a time when only men covered murder and scandal and so she was one of the many women who were assigned to cover the rich and famous. She was bohemian in her dress and liberal in her beliefs. She was private in her life yet so yearned to be public in her thoughts presenting commentaries of the day.

Unfortunately, her beat was limited to shoes, dresses, jewelry, food, and the great loves and marriages of the day – particularly the scandals.

"JRP" stood for J. Rambler Perkins, another writer, but Edna wouldn't dare lift herself to his stature. An aristocrat, world traveler, famous author, and an occasional columnist whose work would always appear on the front page regardless if Edna's essay was about the scandal of the year, JR was trusted by society and all of our secrets were safe with him. I had met him on several occasions, first on a sailing to Europe and then several times in New York when he and my brother William would travel to New York together for a holiday. I was quite fond of JR and of course, had been severely warned of his activities with young and sometimes very young ladies. Yet, as a woman searching, his explicit stories and animated adventures were tantalizing. He studied at Eton College as the son of Ambassador Colonel Lord George Perkins who served as Consular to the Ottoman Empire stationed in Jerusalem and a junker mother from Berlin whose father also served as a Consular to the Turkish Empire. Raised in Jerusalem until he was twelve, he was one of the few young people we knew who had visited the Orient, India, and South America while being educated in an Arab land and at the top universities in England and America. It was his great written works that made him famous and, like so many authors, his notoriety began with one novel published a few years earlier.

The foyer of cultic ruins at the *Skull & Bones* was teeming with Yale officials, New Haven police officers, Vanderbilt

Pinkertons, Chauncey, Inspector Cartwright, and his two subordinates (the raggedy passed over for promotion and often divorced Captain Donnelly, and the recently promoted doer Detective Elmer Grimes). Beyond the granite door was the main hall with columns, carvings, vats, runes, and knights lined against the walls. Windowless, the only light was provided by torches. In the middle was King Cornelius, walking alone and silent. Each step he took on the marble floor echoed throughout the chamber.

As Chauncey and Inspector Cartwright entered the Hall, they were terrified by the scene. The body was in the center of as if it were on display naked with his arms and legs spread tied hanging from the walls in a prostrated position of humiliation. It was immediately apparent that a horrific murder and brutal rape had occurred. The chest to the abdomen was sliced thru and gutted with entrails spilled all over the floor.

"Is this how they found him," asked King Cornelius?

Cartwright, "It is."

The body had been mutilated to such an extent that Chauncey insisted that "the body must be cremated, no pictures ever taken, and no report ever written. No one will ever speak of this". A story had to be created. A heinous murder had occurred. A cover-up now existed that if known at the Court of Astor might cause the House of Vanderbilt to fall.

Perkins had never believed that royal courts in America actually existed. Of course there was always the occasional joke at a party, but no one suspected that it was anything more than a supper society or a group of men smoking cigars in a New York club. It was just one more rumor in a city filled with gossip. The front page of the Daily Herald yesterday covered an expose about another suspect in the Jack the Ripper murders in London. The world had contracted, as more and more people debated world affairs and business, science and medicine, and fashion and art, uniting peoples and populations through the use of new technologies in communication and methods of transportation. Youth were leaving their parents' farms and flocking to the cities in search of success, peace, and prosperity as we prepared to usher in the twentieth century. Despite the boundless future on the horizon, King Cornelius was consumed by his bereavement and concern for succession.

I was certain that Neily would accede as the heir, and by doing so, inherit secrets and the most coveted confidences. William had understood the risk and now he was gone. My heart was ripped apart. Even if he had died of an illness or in battle, what would it matter? My brother was lost.

It was about four in the morning when Edna came rushing into the newsroom and found its occupants entertaining themselves with stogies and whiskey. A little party had broken out as reports were heard of people in long lines waiting for the morning edition at every corner throughout the city. One of the paperboys who usually sold three hundred morning copies had already sold more than two thousand. Two million copies had been printed and everybody at the Daily Herald, which for that day and several thereafter, tripled its circulation, received significant salary bonuses due to their hard work and most importantly for being the only publication in the city with the correct front page headline: "William Vanderbilt Murdered at Yale."

Sunset in the winter in New Haven had always been an emotional cancer for young William. To the east was Newport and to the west was New York City and the connection between the two was his, palpably and righteously. His routine was simple for even as a noble, his only responsibility was his studies. In the summers he and his counterparts would reminisce about their triumphs at school as a charge-D for their hereditary Houses, but each was simply prating. In the fall, the days became shorter, and the nights lengthened the loneliness for the isolated -- abandonment by choice and often not of one's own. The heiress had her problems, the heir had his, but Prince William had them all.

Christmas should have brought some much needed cheer, but, like a drug, it was only a temporary fix, the way down assuredly beginning in the hours after the clocks struck midnight on New Year's Eve. William would cry in pain. At twenty-two years of age he already had a tremendous weight on his shoulders equivalent to a new king of minor age ruling an absolute monarchy without a regent. He was aging quickly and he was cognizant of the grave situation. His hairline was receding and he could not see without spectacles. His appearance, aroma, and actions were of little consequence to him. From dawn until he eventually calmed the compulsive spinning in his brain enough so he could pray to drift away, he believed that the unknown dream was far better than his known obsessive life.

Make no mistake however; he certainly never took anything for granted. He was acutely aware of how bewildering his lifestyle must have appeared to those looking in from the outside. How ridiculous, and in fact how inappropriate it should be for him to have any worry in the world; much less dare express a hint of disappointment looking out from the inside. However, within his subconscious he was a walking corpse. His only hope was that if the heart is powerful enough that the indigent can get through each day with only love, it then explains why he could not get through each day for being denied love.

His story was so simple he could have drawn it in a painting. Only those lucky few who had felt that brief and first moment of love as passion, rather than as friendship, and how it can seduce new thoughts and sensations that they never could even have imagined existed could understand the inverse pain caused both initially, eventually, in small ways and in those completely consuming. Only through love and its eventually assured denial can one truly experience pain and hurt. If there is no rise, there cannot be a fall because it must be compared to something; so without the loss the victory cannot be fully understood. Unfortunately, the two never present themselves in equal part. A little sweet does not mean the inevitable bitter is proportionate. Beware to the romantics that a little high can lead to a great crash. William Vanderbilt had been robbed. He did taste the delicacy but was left with nothing but an acrid aftertaste. His painting was pure bitterness, and only by viewing it at a particular angle could a touch of life be seen. The tinder embers had been decreasing in size, smaller and smaller, as it was extinguishing itself trickling into a lost candle with no flame.

The painting was of a prince and his entourage standing on one side with a damsel and her mistresses on the other. The bottom is bright colors while the top is dark and white. Below are the flowers and the puppies and above are the storms and the unknown and the never explainable genesis of space and time and life. The ground was soothing while the top was ghostly. In the middle was a simple problem that had existed between parent and child forever. He could have a piece, a portion, or all of anything, as all bowed before him, yet the only thing he desired was being denied by his mother. His reaction, surprisingly, was rarely negative and never focused toward Mrs. Vanderbilt. It was a plague hidden within the Palace of the Great Houses. Ironically, his obsession with someone he could never marry was minimized compared to the torture of imagining her bare in the touch of another man.

Grace Wilson, from the House of Astor, was the subject of his infatuation, though she believed that through diplomacy and persistence, Mrs. Vanderbilt could be turned. Her efforts toward reconciliation were misinterpreted by the young Prince William as adoration for him. But most of all it was Grace's narcissism that caused her constant defeats. Like so many times when a man who was in love with Grace would slowly bleed to death in confusion, belittlement and hidden pain. And as before, her disorder prevented Grace from maintaining relationships. Meeting even simple responsibilities, and growing a home both in heart and in brick. Had she not had her riches to support her, she never would have been able to maintain a lover or a house, for the abuser is always focused on her needs and like a drunk she does not care who she hurts so long as the bottom of the flask is never empty. It is an ongoing tale of the victimizer and the abused. The victim believes they are in a relationship while the narcissist just loves the booze and doesn't care what's in the bottle. It will always end in tragedy.

This agony manifested itself several days after the New Year when William, reaching the lowest point in his life, found himself walking through the New Haven Green. The anxiety in his eyes was flaring while the sadness in his breath was aflame. He couldn't understand why his soul abdicated nor why his brain's electrical charge waned -- by now he was only a corpse; an emaciated torso, stagnate knees, frozen organs, and paralyzed limbs. As he reached High Street, he had to turn left or right, because standing before him was the *Skull & Bones* oubliette. The fog that had descended onto the campus that morning had by dusk become thunder echoing over Long Island Sound. Finally, something refreshing – a slight humid icy breeze to break this febrile man – even if only for a moment.

Silence broke the humdrum of the crashing heavens as they began to scatter moving further up the coast and out to sea. AND THEN – Looking down the Angels were alarmed as young William had not been expected. Free will left and to the right divinity of fate. He glanced left and noticed steps leading down. On the right, the gardens were calming the green quad. Left death or right life. The forces to move to the beyond overpowered, and as the princely eyes gazed left his body helplessly seemed to follow.

At the bottom was a faint light brightening step by step that once reached, the light would blow out his earthly life like the flicker of a suffocating candle. Now hopeless -- consciously or subconsciously -- powerless, his hourglass was foundering. Beseeching, the Angels trembled pleading for compurgation.

A breath, subtle in its inhale, exhales to a slight smile on William's face upon hearing the heavenly chorus. The Angels are stunned, since eternity their screams never realized that they could even be heard. In awe, they gather William on their chariots and like a shepherd pasturing his flock, avowing the sheep to pass under his staff, so too is William. Triumphant, the Angels flew away.

"AHHHHH"

William was stabbed. He gagged helplessly lifting his head. He was not ready to die; he had chosen life. His assailant pushed the knife deeper into his abdomen so that the tip came out his back. He was motionless. His body only reflexing as it perished. His eyes quivered allowing only blurred vision.

"You learned the secret, so now you shall die with the secret," said the murderer.

With only seconds left in his life, rather than recall a nice moment, a friend, or a prayer he understood and was not surprised when the executioner quickly pulled the hunting knife out of his body and just as quickly shoved it back in, this time with a smile on her face that she made sure William saw.

Lady X was pleased as she watched William Vanderbilt bleed to death before her. As he was hemorrhaging, she kept him fixed upright looking into his eyes. So sadistic was she that she could not control herself as the sexual mania was overpowering.

Wearing a full body devilish red cloak she opened it revealing shiny black leather dominatrix attire. He was shaking in death. She attempted to keep her eyes open but the moisture of her kill was reaching her inner breaking point. Succumbing, her knees gave way and they spread apart opening herself to receive her kill. At that moment she could no longer control her masochism and finished at the same time William's life slipped from the Earth and returned to the Angel's chariots which were not far away.

A new fog swirled about like the ghosts of Lady X's previous prey. As William's corpse lay there on the side of the dirt road she closed her cloak. She swiveled her head in a circular motion expressing power by cracking the aches in her neck. She was proud of her new submissive and his fulfillment to her was now complete. She reached down and pulled the dagger out of his body and placed it back in her cloak. She then snapped her fingers and as she walked away, a gang of hooded men wearing black cloaks and masks moved past her and picked up William's lifeless body.

The Commodore

*The climax is always the beginning
which is the greatest paradox*

The year was One Thousand Eight Hundred and Seventy Seven. The month was January. The date was the fourth. For seven years the engineers who designed the Brooklyn Bridge had achieved one transportation marvel after the next, though it would take 7 more years before it would be completed.

Not far away, at 10 Washington Place stood a five story townhouse in the midst of a row of others that appeared simple compared to the American palaces that would be built twenty years later. Outside, the entire street was closed off, as crowds from afar gathered on the neighboring streets. As was customary at any Vanderbilt estate in times to come, police officers and security guards were keeping reporters and the crowds at bay on this piece of Manhattan Island. A post "White Christmas" snow was falling and covered the many carriages lining the street and it was on this date and at this place that the Vanderbilt Pinkertons assembled for the first time to protect the first American king. Something momentous was happening here, with American soldiers arriving overnight.

"I think I'm nearly gone, Doctor," were the words whispered softly by an elderly tall, thin, and grey Cornelius Vanderbilt lying in bed. In contrast to the 82 year old dying man, his second wife Frankie Crawford, was 38, not even half his age. She was joined by his son William Henry Vanderbilt, several of the city's most knowledgeable doctors, and a delegation of government officials, generals, and lawyers, who were there to bear witness.

They surrounded this first American royal to offer prayers. "Now may the peace of God which passeth all understanding keep your hearts and minds on Christ Jesus; and the blessing of God Almighty, the Father, the Son, and the Holy Ghost."

"God damn good prayer, I say."

Frankie asked, "Your children are all outside, should I bring them in?"

"I don't need them. I got Billy here."

"Well what about all the grandchildren then? They can come in and sing."

The Commodore nodded in the affirmative and with what little strength he had left, strained to smile. Frankie waved and the servants opened the doors to allow his grandchildren and great grandchildren to fill the room. From the hallway outside, an organist played "Come Ye Sinners, Poor, and Needy" as the Commodore moved his head slightly from side to side. By the second stanza his lips began to move.

Mrs. Vanderbilt

Come, Ye thirsty, Come and welcome
God's free bounty glorify.
True belief and true repentance
Every grace that brings you nigh.

Come, Ye weary, Heavy-laden.
Lost and ruined by the fall.
If you tarry 'til you're better.
You will never come at all.

I will arise and go to Jesus.
He will embrace me in His arms.
In the arms of my Saviour,
O, There are ten thousand charms.

He soon fell behind the others; the Commodore repeating the refrain, "I am poor, I am needy, weak and wounded, sick and sore."

One last time, the first American King opened his eyes, looked up at his son Billy, and said, "When I pass you'll be told a secret. Never reveal it to outsiders I say. Keep the money together, my boy. Keep it away from them. Keep the New York Central our road. Keep it together. You're my only son, Billy."

The Commodore closed his eyes and passed. What he should have said was that Billy was the only living son he trusted. In actuality, the Commodore had four sons: one Wise, one Wicked, one Simple and one who didn't know how to ask.

The "one who didn't know how to ask" barely knew how to speak when he died in the fourth year of life. He was named for the great American hero and first President of the United States, General George Washington, so when the Commodore's last child, a son, was born several years after the toddler's death, he too was named George Washington. This second George Washington was the source of the Commodore's pride and joy and proved to the cynics that the Commodore had a heart, and possibly felt something for somebody other than himself. Fortuitously, the Simple son always brightened everything he touched until he died childless in the Civil War.

In Europe when one king died, another was crowned in his place, and so too the House of Vanderbilt would pass from one generation to another. Anticipating the inevitable, the obituaries had already been written, the funeral planned and rehearsed, the eulogies perfected, and every minute from Cornelius Vanderbilt's last breath until he was laid to rest on Staten Island had been staged and would be performed for the eyes of the world as a state funeral.

While the grandchildren and great grandchildren touched their grand papa for the last time, smelled him, saw him, and felt his presence, in the drawing room just outside the bedroom the Commodore's children sat on lavish sofas, drank the finest scotch, and filled the room with pipe smoke.

One of the Commodore's eight daughters, Mary Alicia, broke the silence by scolding her brother Corneel, "It's not even 10:30 and our father lies dying in the next room. Must you drink?"

"Must you be an ass?"

Another daughter, Ethelinda asked, "Why is only Billy allowed to see him?"

Mary Alicia responded, "Because, Corneel here can't go a day without drinking or gambling, or whatever it is that you do."

And yet another daughter chimed in, "Do you really think Billy's going to take over the company?"

Mary Alicia clarified her position, "Sophia, I don't want the company. I just want my inheritance."

For miles horse drawn carriages lined the roads of Staten Island and all flags in New York City flew at half-mast. The funeral cortege passed onlookers rich and poor, old and young, as the procession entered the cemetery. One New York newspaper wrote, "It was a giant they buried. An old sea captain who had known him well said that it was fortunate that the Commodore had not received any formal education, for if he had, he would have been a God". Whether he was a God or not I don't know, but he died the richest man in the world.

Even as a two year old girl who can't remember him except for what she has seen in pictures, I knew he was important to my father. William Henry Vanderbilt, my grand papa, was special to me so the Commodore must have been special to my father. He was, after all, his namesake.

The Commodore was known for having a wild vocabulary and rarely held back. Everyone knew what he thought of them and he knew what they thought of him, but he didn't care. Ironic for a man who was so blunt and direct in life, that it was only in death that he would shock the world, and particularly the Vanderbilt family.

Within hours after the funeral, Judge Charles Rapallo called together the Commodore's wife Frankie, and his nine spuriously grieving children for the reading of the will: Phebe, Ethelinda, Eliza, Emily, Sophia, Maria Louisa, Mary Alicia, Catherine Jouliette, Corneel, and Billy. Also in attendance were the Commodore's four grandsons: my father Corneilus II (34 years old), Alva's husband William Henry (Willie, 28 years old), Fredrick William who would die after a long childless life (21), and George Washington II who became famous for building the Biltmore Estate in Asheville, North Carolina (15), all standing next to their father. Frankie was sitting on a sofa with Billy, while the others were all standing, as there were no other chairs. Judge Rapallo began reading:

The principal heir to my fortune shall be my son William Henry Vanderbilt, with the following exclusions. My wife, Frankie, shall receive five hundred thousand dollars and my house at 10 Washington Place. My daughters Mesdames Cross, Thorn, Clark, Torrance, and La Bau shall receive two hundred and fifty thousand dollars each. My daughter Mrs. Osgood shall receive three hundred thousand dollars. My daughter Mrs. Allen shall receive four hundred thousand dollars. My daughter Mrs. Lafitte shall receive five hundred thousand dollars. My son Cornelius Jeremiah Vanderbilt shall receive two hundred thousand dollars to be held in trust so he doesn't lose it gambling. My grandson Cornelius II, shall *receive $5.5 million dollars in stock and cash. William Henry's three other sons, William, Fredrick, and George Washington, shall each receive $2 million dollars in stock and cash.*

The judge continued, "The other part that he insisted I read to you word for word was this."

All the rest, residue, and remainder of the property and estate, real and personal, of every description and where-so-ever situated of which I may be possessed, and to which I may be entitled at the time of my demise, I give, devise, and bequeath unto my son William H. Vanderbilt.

Infuriated, Mary Alicia lashed out, "Billy, you had Chauncey write that, didn't you? Father could not speak like that, let alone write like that."

"Mr. Vanderbilt," the judge continued, "also left $300,000 to be divided amongst these 22 people," as he passed out a list which Marry Alicia grabbed and quickly read, "The pastor gets $25,000?"

Ethelinda, "Billy, you son of a bitch."

Corneel, "You sold us out."

Frankie yelled, "Enough everybody!"

Mary Alicia, "You're not our mother. You're our cousin who bedded our father."

With his son Cornelius right behind him, Billy rose and walked toward Mary Alicia and looked her straight in the eye, "Get out of this house!"

"I'll see you in court," yelled Mary Alicia as she walked out and slammed the door. Corneel and the other sisters soon followed. The conversation between Billy and Frankie was cordial. Billy and his four sons thanked the judge.

No sooner had the last person left the room, when Billy and his sons began opening bottles of champagne. Billy said to them, "I need all of you. Cornelius, you're now first vice president, and you and Willie will be on the board of the New York Central. Fredrick and George, if you want to work for the company you're more than welcome, but I will not require it."

Young George, "Thank you, father."

Cornelius II, concluded with a toast, "God bless our grandfather."

In all, the newly anointed King William Henry Vanderbilt inherited $95,000,000 and his sons more than $10,000,000. The Commodore had set in motion that the Vanderbilt Empire would pass from his son William Henry to his grandson, the new heir apparent, Prince Cornelius and eventually to his eldest son, who should have been my brother William Henry, though after his untimely death, Neily became the de facto eldest son. In its size, the Vanderbilt inheritance could only be compared to the Astor fortune which was only worth $40,000,000. The jubilation however, would be short lived.

By May of 1877, only five months later, railroad workers in Pittsburgh were walking off the job and flooding the streets in what was one of America's first labor strikes organized by the union movement. The crowds soon grew in numbers.

The signs read, "Pay us $1.00 a day." The rail workers began burning passenger cars and depots with their torches.

It would be a real tragedy if future generations believed that the Victorians on the east coast of America were enlightened. They were the descendants of the first generations of American citizens and believed in American exceptionalism expressed through religious freedom, commercial exploits, and immunity from European royal decrees. Was the progression of society propelled by the Victorians or in spite of them?

The challenge for America was that the lessons gleaned from Europe were not learned by us through our own national experiences. We knew what we didn't want in King George's England, but since most of the revolutionaries were born in America, we were immersed in independence without understanding the accountability that accompanied it. We simply took what we did not like over there and tried to start anew over here. The feudal system had been abolished in Europe long ago while a modern form in America, lacking any historical practice, had been developing for several generations. In the South there were plantations and in the North there were mills. The owner of the plantation was responsible for housing his slaves just as the owner of the mill was responsible for housing his workers.

In New York the Grand Central Station was the heart of the Vanderbilt empire. In addition to the thousands of passengers seeking first class transcontinental travel, the lawyers, businessmen, and doctors holding second class tickets, and the third class immigrant families who were travelling west in search of a new beginning, the station was crowded with the Pinkertons and police officers on patrol to protect the Vanderbilt's source of income. For years prior, the Commodore had maintained a simple office with several clerks; his strongest traits were not administrative, mathematical, or engineering, nor had he ever read any piece of paper that was longer than half a page, but he was successful for three reasons. He did it first, he did it the best, and he was crooked – all the signs of an obsessively competitive personality. For the Svengali in the Commodore, Billy had all the necessary business skills, an excellent memory and attention to detail, and while also competitive, he was a master tactician. Though not the original "Crown Prince," Billy developed his edge when his father sent him to run a bankrupt Staten Island railroad which he turned into one of the most profitable lines in the country. Chauncey was the General to Billy's Admiral so when he burst into the office out of breath, he quickly drew the attention of Billy and his two sons, Cornelius and Willie.

His first words, "We just received word that the Erie, Baltimore, and Ohio railroads are all striking."

Willie was first to respond, "Interesting. Astor's workers are striking."

Chauncey, catching his breath, "Angry mobs have torched hundreds of cars and locomotives and ripped apart the tracks."

The new head of the House of Vanderbilt offered, "Times are tough for everyone. Our workers are loyal and they can afford to take the same 10% pay cuts that Astor is forcing on his bunch. To stay competitive, we cannot pay our laborers more than Astor is. I told the stockholders and bond holders, who; might I add, are in favor of the 10% cut, that today a Vanderbilt rail worker makes the equivalent of a barrel of flour each day, and that is more than enough."

Of the two sons, Cornelius' strategic wisdom inquired, "what of the lawsuit by Uncle Corneel and your sisters?"

Billy responded, "Chauncey is managing it. Who are you bringing in?"

"The brilliant criminal lawyer Henry Clinton, and former chief justice of the New York court of appeals, George Comstock."

Cornelius, "Father, what is the benefit of initiating this action? Why take the risk of having the men strike?"

Chauncey responded, "My sense is if it's being asked of other men, then the Vanderbilt workers can afford it. We're not a charity here. Let me remind you that last year we had earnings of just under $30,000,000, and after expenses the Central only netted $12,000,000. As far as I'm concerned, we should proceed with the wage cut."

Billy, "Chauncey is right. What do these workers need more money for anyway?"

Cornelius, "Father, just don't let anyone hear you say something like that. Remember, the money to feed one of your horses for a day is more than their daily wage. The women get half that and a child five cents. Ten if they are lucky."

Chauncey, "Regardless, don't you think the men will strike and destroy the Grand Central?"

Billy, "Not at all. I place great confidence in our men. My great trust in them is founded on their intelligent appreciation of the business situation at the present time. Their hope, like ours, is for better times. Our stock is falling. We need to reward the stockholders rather than the workers if we want the stock price to rise."

Cornelius concluded, "So the decision is final. Chauncey, inform management to cut workers' pay by ten percent."

Billy, "Cornelius, Willie, I'm counting on you to make sure we stay focused on expansion and acquisitions. It's the only way we can stay competitive with Astor. Chauncey, join me for a moment."

As the two entered Billy's private office, "I need you to hire a private investigator to follow Corneel. Get evidence about the drinking and the gambling and the women -- especially the women. How much will it cost?"

Chauncey thought before replying, "$5,000 to start."

Billy walked over to the wall and moved a painting two reveal a safe in the wall which he opened and from which he took $5,000 two hand to Chauncey.

Chauncey, "I've been courting a new operative that may just be right for the job"

Billy, "Great."

"But she's a woman, a very young woman."

"How young?"

"Young enough that she keeps the page boys working for nothing"

"And how does she do that?"

"She's sixteen and most of the pages are thirteen or fourteen, some even younger."

"Is she intimate with them?"

"Think of her more as a mole. She uses her beauty to gather information about our employees, not just the lads but their fathers. I've been thinking about giving her a more important assignment."

"What's her name?"

"The boys call her Lady X."

"I want to meet her"

The Moon was bright. The air was clear. The station was small. Near Nyack, north of New York City along the Hudson River, several people were waiting to board the train. Over 30 cars in length, pulled by two locomotives, the train sounded its horns as it entered the station. Emerging from the smoke of the steam engine a woman with long black hair wearing a black cloak with her face covered by a black veil quickly boarded the train.

Lady X enjoyed her first class setting as a servant handed her a glass of champagne and presented her with a note. She read it, took a final sip from her glass, leaving a bright red lipstick stain and stood up. She walked toward the front of the car which was filled with ostentatiously dressed passengers, drinking, smoking, eating, gambling, all while listening to a four piece orchestra. The woman approached the front of the car where two Vanderbilt guards blocked the door. As she approached they stood aside and on cue opened the door.

She entered a car decorated in that served as a foyer to the King's royal car Louis XV style. Two more Vanderbilt guards dressed in suits were sitting on each side of the door. They both rose as she entered. At the other end of the car, two footmen in red livery stood on each side of the door. Chauncey was the only other person in the car. As he motioned her over she passed him the footmen opened the private family car.

The next coach was also decorated in Louis XV style with a fire burning in a specially constructed fireplace. Priceless paintings cover the walls with others carefully placed on the floor, as there was no wall space left. The furniture was abundant and cramped the car which only had one passenger; Billy sitting at his desk, drinking tea and reviewing stacks of business records

Lady X entered the coach and closed the door. Billy rose from his chair as she walked over to him and took off her coat. Billy bent down and picked up a briefcase from under his desk. When he looked back, her coat was off and she was removing her veil.

Billy opened the briefcase. It was filled with packs of $100 bills that appeared to be newly printed. He began handing her packets of bills.

Without regard for the other passengers, the train gradually slowed down in the middle of the upstate New York countryside. Lady X exited the car, and with the Vanderbilt guards helping her across the tracks, she entered a private two car train heading back to Manhattan. As the trains began to separate; Lady X considered her new assignment while the

Vanderbilt train blew its steam heading back through the mountains on its way north to Saratoga for the summer season of 1877.

Several weeks later, King Billy Vanderbilt and his son Prince Cornelius II were having dinner seated at a very long grand table that could easily seat a grand party. Several footmen standing at the alert were caught with such surprise that one almost dropped the serving dish on Cornelius as Chauncey burst agitated and breathless into the room.

"Mr. Vanderbilt, we have an emergency. Our men are striking and threatening to burn down the Grand Central."

"That damn Astor is using his men to influence our workers."

Chauncey continued, "In Pittsburgh, President Hayes sent in the army after the workers overtook the state militia. Sir, we should explore a different approach, in light of what happened in France with King Louis."

"What do you propose?"

"We need to act quickly. We currently have eleven thousand employees and most would probably agree to a 5% give back with the other 5% to follow in six months if the economy improves."

Billy pondered the suggestion, "On average, we pay each worker 90¢ a day, so if we do what you suggest every worker will make a dollar. My lawyers and bankers each already earn $10,000 a year. Chauncey, can we really afford this?"

"We're simply restoring wages to where they were last year."

Billy asked, "Do you think they will agree?"

"I believe we should add an incentive."

"Really?"

Chauncey clarifies, "A bonus."

"How much?"

"$100,000 to be shared by all eleven thousand workers."

Billy's facial expression conveyed the impression that someone had stolen all his money. Seeing this Chauncey quickly added, "The average bonus will be $12.00 and it is only a one-time thing."

Billy, "Don't be naïve. It's not a one-time thing. We cannot establish a precedent of acquiescing to the workers' demands every time they strike. If they don't want to work for me, let them find wages elsewhere. For each worker, there are twenty that would happily take their place."

Chauncey, "Well then, let's not allow everyone to return to work."

"No?"

"They must learn that any raise will cost them as well. We must inform all of them and those that follow that a wage increase will result, in fact must result, in the company being forced to fire others in order to afford it."

Cornelius questioned, "But, that's not true. We can afford it and keep all of our workers."

Chauncey, "That is correct, but they don't know it. If we do it once and other companies follow our lead, the people will believe it to be true. Regardless, in a generation automation will make the worker obsolete just as electricity has made kerosene irrelevant."

Billy was convinced, "If it costs $100,000, then pay it and let's get back to work."

In the end, while King Billy was fighting his estranged brother Corneel over their father's $100,000,000 will, he wisely settled with the workers for a mere $100,000. The incident soon passed and Chauncey was viewed as brilliant amongst his peers for convincing Billy to end the strike. The men of the New York Central returned to work and the Vanderbilts' money machine continued like a printing press, pouring in cash by the millions.

Perkins would later write that Billy had drawn a line in the sand as if he were closing a curtain – a curtain over the poor and the common man. If the Gilded Age became notorious for the gild then too the curtain was recognized as being blind. The Blind Curtain, you know it is there, you can't see it, you don't know what it means, all you know is that it is evil yet all you see is the good. It is whatever you want and whatever you fear. It is what you perceive it to be regardless of what it really is. We live in a dream only because our reality is so horrible. What we admire the most is exactly what wants us to fail. Who we want to be is who we hate and we don't even realize we're being used. $1.00 a day. What's next? Should we send children to school rather than work in our factories and mills. Is the commoner to pursue rights for women and Negros. The aristocrat can only maintain his wealth through *schadenfreude*. It is not just enough to succeed but in order to do so others must fail and the aristocrat must feel great joy and pride in witnessing such demise or he cannot implement such horror. And the only way to achieve this is through the Blind Curtain -- the paradoxical curtain -- where one side is blinded by the truth while the other side keeps the curtain closed. Being rich isn't as hard as keeping others from being rich. The cynic would say that if everyone is rich then no one is truly wealthy. Then the rich have become common and that is when the Blind Curtain opens finally for everyone so that the greater light can be seen and lived by all.

November 12, 1878 was the first day of one of the most sensational trials over which a judge ever presided in an American court. Almost two years after the Commodore died, in Surrogate Judge Delano Calvin's courtroom, US Congressman Scott Lord and former Chief justice of the Supreme Court of Pennsylvania Jeremiah Black arrived first, to arrive with their client Corneel Vanderbilt in the case of Corneel, Ethelinda Allen, and Marie Alicia La Bau versus their brother William Kissam Vanderbilt and his four sons. The stakes were one hundred million and it was called "the trial of the century" with Perkins reporting daily the dramatic testimony and its witnesses.

The area around the court house on Chambers Street was crowded with spectators who were being controlled by police officers trying to maintain order. Coaches made their way through the blocked off streets and stopped just outside the courthouse where attorneys Scott Lord and Jeremiah Black emerged, followed by Corneel Vanderbilt. The arrival of King Billy and his entourage made his brother's arrival appear meager by comparison. It was a royal procession.

Inside the courtroom, there was standing room only. Police officers and Vanderbilt Pinkertons encircled the room and newspaper reporters made up half the crowd. The defendants and plaintiffs were seated in their appointed places and behind them were the Vanderbilts' servants, valets and footmen as the gild was as important as the proceeding itself. Although Chauncey had organized the legal strategy, Billy's sons' Cornelius II, Willie, Fredrick, and George Vanderbilt had a ceremonial role to fill.

Seated at the Plaintiff's table were Corneel, Mary Alicia La Bau, and Ethelinda Allen and attorneys Lord and Black. At the Defendant's table, Billy sat next to his lead attorneys Henry Clinton and George Comstock, surrounded by other less senior Vanderbilt attorneys.

Everyone rose from their seats as Judge Delano Calvin entered. He began the proceeding, "Are you ready gentlemen?"

Mr. Clinton stood, "Ready on behalf of the defendants."

Mr. Lord followed, "We're ready sir."

"Proceed gentleman."

Mr. Lord began, "Cornelius Vanderbilt, known to all of us as the great Commodore, was not like you and me, not just because he was the richest man in the world, but because he was a man who pursued married women, married his cousin, lived in a second childhood fantasy world and, believed in unorthodox spiritual clairvoyance as a means to pervert Providence."

He pointed directly at Billy, "This man William Henry Vanderbilt, rolling in his nearly one hundred million dollars said nearly a quarter century ago that he meant to control his father, showing that even then he had an eye on the disposition of his father's property after death. We have thought it proper to show that the Commodore was in a condition to be influenced, that he suffered from terrible diseases, and that they so affected his mind that he was successful to undue influence. The evidence we have collected shall demonstrate that either the testator created his will while factoring from delusions regarding those for whom the law provides equality of distribution, or else that his mind, although capable of focusing on his railroad projects by force of habit was, due to over-indulgence, delusional and diseased and so impaired that he was subjected to, and acted in making the will under the undue influence and control the residuary, the legatee, William Henry Vanderbilt."

Outraged, Henry Clinton rose from his chair, "The Counsel has said in his opening statement what we believe to be the grossest of slanders."

"Lead counsel should put that in his summation. I'll answer him there," responded Mr. Lord.

The judge, "I do not propose to pass upon the propriety or impropriety of the opening statement."

Mr. Clinton continued with his objection, "It was such an opening as I have never heard in all my experience in courts, and hope never to hear again."

Arguing back Mr. Lord said, "Just because he has $100,000,000 behind him, the counselor will not have to travel far, for the lines amassing against his client go around the block."

Mr. Clinton continued, "If we possess wealth of money on our side, you possess wealth of imagination on yours."

Irritated, Mr. Lord, "I can stand that, considering the source it comes from."

Rolling his eyes, Mr. Clinton, "I can hardly believe anyone outside of a insane asylum would believe the statements made in your opening."

The judge calmly lifted his hands, "Gentlemen, these side remarks had better cease. This case will not be decided upon an opening statement nor upon a summation, but upon the facts as given in evidence."

The onlookers did not fit into the courtroom. The press presence was massive. With Judge Calvin presiding, the public greatly anticipated Corneel Vanderbilt word, while being questioned by Mr. Clinton, "Please tell the court how much was necessary for the support of your family on the farm in Connecticut?"

"I suppose $200 a month would have kept us from starving, but we had to live a proper life costs five or six thousand dollars a year."

"The average mill worker earns $300 a year and lives on it. Meanwhile you think it right to live at a rate of five or six thousand a year on an income of $2,400? It is correct that that was your annual income, was it not?"

Corneel answered "It was."

"Did you accumulate a debt for the difference?"

"I did, I had too. My father forced on me that style of living. I could not turn people away from the house when they came. It was expected of me that I should act in accordance with the Vanderbilt name, which I did."

Clinton continued, "You have stated that you never contracted a debt that you did not intend to repay. Now, from what source did you expect to get this money?"

"From the same source that my brother Billy got his."

"Did you expect to pay them before your father's death?"

"Yes, I expected that he would put me in business and give me the opportunity to earn it," responded Corneel.

"Do you remember anybody with whom you have become acquainted casually that you have not tried to borrow money from?" The courtroom chuckled.

"Yes, thousands of people."

"Has there ever been a month in which you did not incur debt far beyond what your income was?"

Corneel answered, "There have been several months in which I gave no notes and borrowed no money."

"Can you mention any one large city in the nation in which you have not borrowed money and then not paid it back?"

Corneel looked puzzled so Mr. Clinton reiterated, "Again, Mr. Vanderbilt, can you name any American city in which you borrowed money and then failed to pay it back?"

Corneel, "Utica, Rochester, Cincinnati,"

"Any other cities in which you owe money?"

"San Francisco and Philadelphia."

"Well Mr. Vanderbilt, is there a state in the union in which you haven't borrowed money?"

Corneel did not answer him. Mr. Clinton continued, "How much money do you currently owe?"

"Approximately one hundred thousand dollars."

"And of that, how much do you owe to Mr. Horace Greeley?"

Corneel explained, "I told him I might die, and in that event, my father might be so happy that he would be willing to pay off what I owed him."

Mr. Clinton interrupted, "Move to strike your honor."

The Judge, "It is so."

Mr. Lord rose from his chair, "Your honor, if we could be heard on this issue?"

The judge answered, "No, Mr. Lord. You can challenge during summation. Mr. Clinton, you may proceed."

Mr. Clinton continued, "Is it true that you owe Mr. Terry $30,000?"

"Yes. But that money was advanced personally to me and my wife, and he has notes signed by my wife and myself. Since my wife's death, he has given me nothing though and I don't understand why not."

"For what did you use that $30,000? For gambling?"

"I don't think I did. For various things. For paying my debts."

Mr. Clinton pressed him harder, "Is it not true that you have been arrested by criminal authorities more than 40 times for forgery, writing bad checks, and indebtedness?"

"Arrested?"

"Were you in jail?"

"I think I was in jail."

Not seeming to get a direct answer Mr. Clinton attempted to clarify, "Don't you know what is meant by criminal authorities?"

"It is hard to tell what is criminal these days."

"Were you arrested on a criminal warrant and lodged in jail, yes or no?"

"Yes."

"Was not the greatest part of your indebtedness caused by your gambling?"

"No sir, nothing of any great amount was caused in that way, merely a few thousand dollars."

"Have you ever borrowed money from professional gamblers?"

"I have borrowed money from time to time from men that play cards. But I would not pay off gambling debts with that money."

"No, you would just gamble with it," as sarcasm was added by Mr. Clinton.

Mr. Lord, "Objection."

The judge, "Sustained."

Mr. Clinton continued, "Is it true that you pawned your wife's jewelry to feed your gambling addiction?"

"I don't know if I did that for that purpose."

"Did you pawn your wife's jewelry and dresses, yes or no?"

"No, never her dresses."

"Did you pawn her jewelry?"

Corneel explained, "I was in debt frequently and she gave me her jewelry to pay off her debts and some of mine."

"Did you pawn them when she was not willing to give them to you?"

Corneel responded, "She did not appear to be unwilling."

"Do you remember when your brother George died?"

"I do."

"Do you remember some cuff links belonging to him which were given to you?"

"I do. They were given to me by my mother."

"Did you pawn them to raise money to gamble with?"

Corneel, "I pawned them, and when I went to redeem them, I found Billy had gone and gotten them and he never gave them back, although I offered money for them."

"Mr. Vanderbilt, one final question just so your testimony is clear. Isn't it true that you were arrested for forgery and indebtedness by criminal authorities more than 40 times and spent many nights in jail, a jail with bars on the windows? Just so you understand what jail is."

Corneel, "I don't know what I did. I won't swear that I didn't."

"Mr. Vanderbilt, I don't know what any of your testimony means."

Mr. Lord interrupted, "Objection."

Everyone in the courtroom giggled. The judge wished he had never been assigned to this case. "Mr. Lord, relax, relax. To be perfectly honest, I don't understand what his testimony means either."

"Objection!" Mr. Lord slammed his fist on the desk as the Judge, with one finger from both hands motioned both counselors into his chambers.

What started as a case about money quickly turned into a case about vices, corruption, and innuendo. The courtroom was filled with attorneys, spectators, and reporters from around the world eagerly awaiting the next scandal to be revealed, as Judge Calvin, Mr. Lord, and Mr. Clinton continued their discussion behind closed doors.

The Judge asked, "Mr. Lord, what do you propose?"

"We have just learned that Mr. Clinton plans to introduce the results of a secret investigation conducted by a private investigator hired by Mr. William Vanderbilt and his associate Mr. Chauncey Depew."

Mr. Clinton interrupted, "Mr. Lord was informed weeks ago of this investigation. He has deposed the investigator and there is no reason why this testimony should not be offered. On countless occasions the investigator observed Corneel Vanderbilt gambling in high class casinos, drinking and fornicating every night, visiting brothels – must I go on. The jury is entitled to hear that testimony."

The judge, "I agree, Mr. Lord."

Mr. Lord, "Your honor, we can prove through direct testimony that this investigator was specifically hired to discredit Corneel Vanderbilt in the eyes of his father, which led to him being excluded from the Commodore's will."

The judge interrupted, "Hiring an investigator is within the defendant's rights."

Mr. Lord continued, "We believe that this was a conspiracy concocted by the defendants and that the investigators were following the wrong person."

"Balderdash!" yelled Mr. Clinton.

The Judge, "Mr. Lord, are you suggesting that Mr. Vanderbilt and Mr. Depew hired an actor to parade around the city as a drunken fool so that his actions could be witnessed by the investigators and that it was those findings upon which the dying Commodore Vanderbilt relied when he excluded the plaintiff from his will?"

"That's exactly what I'm suggesting and that all findings from the investigation simply be ruled inadmissible by your honor. We're not arguing whether Mr. Vanderbilt and Mr. Depew are necessarily culpable, although we believe that to be the case."

Mr. Clinton looked at Mr. Lord stone faced, "Are you inebriated?"

The Judge chuckled.

Mr. Lord continued, "Regardless of whether they hired a look-a-like double or not, the defense cannot prove that the investigator was actually following Corneel Vanderbilt and the investigators testimony will prejudice the jury."

The Judge decided, "I'll let the jury hear it all. However, Mr. Lord, do not suggest something about Mr. William Vanderbilt or Mr. Depew unless you review your witness with me first. You shall both have an opportunity to question the investigator."

Smiling and trying to hide his chuckle, Mr. Clinton concluded, "Thank you your honor."

Back in the courtroom everyone was in their usual seats as the trial continued. The investigator, Mr. Redburn, was on the stand.

Mr. Lord proceeded with his questioning, "Can you positively say that it was this man here, Mr. Corneel Vanderbilt, that you claim to have seen going in and out of these clubs?"

Mr. Redburn responded, "Yes, it's definitely him."

"Is it possible that you saw someone who looked like him?"

"No, it's definitely him."

"Is it possible that you saw someone you thought was Mr. Corneel Vanderbilt, but could have in fact been a person deceiving you by dressing like and behaving in the same manner as Mr. Vanderbilt?"

Mr. Clinton jumped up, "Your honor."

The Judge, "Mr. Lord, I warned you. Unless you can produce for this court a witness that can substantiate these outrageous claims, you are ordered to move on."

Mr. Lord continued, "Your honor, we are in fact subpoenaing two Vanderbilt footmen who claim to have seen a woman enter Mr. Vanderbilt's private train car, leave with a bag full of cash, and board a train to Manhattan with the instruction to hire a Corneel Vanderbilt look-a-like even after the passing of Commodore Vanderbilt."

Mr. Clinton, "This is outrageous. Your honor, he's prejudicing the jury."

Mr. Lord continued, "Further these gentlemen will offer direct testimony that it was in fact this same woman dressed as a man whom Mr. Redburn followed during his investigation in the late months of 1876 and not my client."

Mr. Clinton interrupted, "Your honor, the jury should be hearing this from the witnesses, not from Mr. Lord, unless of course he saw this mysterious person himself."

Everyone in the courtroom laughed. The judge banged his gavel and directed his annoyance at Mr. Lord, "Enough, the two of you. Mr. Lord you are ordered to produce these witnesses tomorrow morning."

Mr. Clinton, "He can't because they don't exist."

Angrily the Judge, "If these witnesses are not in my court room you will be held in contempt and I will make it quite clear to the jury why you'll be spending a night in jail – and I mean a jail with bars on the window."

As the observers anticipated the continuation of the circus before them, Judge Calvin ordered Mr. Clinton and Mr. Lord back into his chamber. No sooner had they entered the judge slammed the door and Mr. Clinton started, "Your honor, the defense moves for an immediate mistrial."

Mr. Lord asked, "Why, because your client bribes half of New York?"

Clinton responded, "At least he doesn't owe money in every state in the union and on the seven continents. In fact, if your client could travel to Mars he would owe money to a Martian."

The Judge asked, "Enough the two of you. What's your argument Mr. Clinton?"

"The jury has been prejudiced to a point beyond legal repair. Perjured commentary by Mr. Lord has slandered the character of my client."

Mr. Lord, "As if that was so difficult."

The Judge offered his opinion, "Mr. Lord, I'm inclined to believe that the witnesses, if they exist, will offer perjured testimony. As I understand your argument, you want me to believe a story about a woman in a cloak jumping from train to train with a bundle of pay-off cash she a received from Mr. Vanderbilt, and then hiring a stage actor to get drunk and gamble, all the while pretending to be Corneel Vanderbilt. Truly, Mr. Lord, how much of this do you expect me to believe? It's beyond the pale. Remember, the Commodore didn't just exclude Corneel, he essentially excluded all of his children except for Mr. William Vanderbilt. Mr. Lord, you have a tough hill ahead. I suggest a settlement is in everyone's best interest. Mr. Clinton? You first."

Mr. Clinton realized the Judge was on his side, though he knew he had to offer something reasonable to keep the Judge there. He offered, "$500,000."

From a clearly weakened position Mr. Lord responded, "Your honor, we really want to continue with the trial."

The Judge wanted a settlement, "A number please, Mr. Lord?"

"One million dollars, for each."

Clinton laughed, "He's crazy your honor. There is no way Mr. Vanderbilt will ever agree to anything except if it is in trust. Otherwise, what is to prevent him from coming again and again and asking for more and more. It's never going to happen. Not even Chauncey will be able to convince him."

The Judge, "Well, what about the two sisters? Mr. Clinton?"

"Half a million each - - not a dime more."

The Judge looked at Mr. Lord who nodded his head in the affirmative, "Done."

The Judge, "And what about Corneel?"

As the three men exited the judge's private chamber and took their places in the courtroom, Mr. Clinton motioned to Chauncey indicating that a settlement had been reached. Once he sat beside him, he whispered, "We've settled with Mary Alicia and Ethelinda."

Chauncey asked, "For how much?"

"$500,000 each."

"In the name of God!" Billy was shocked.

Mr. Clinton explained, "It could be a great deal worse. It gives us leverage with Corneel. His attorney will agree to a trust but Corneel is going to demand some cash too."

"How much?"

Mr. Clinton's suggested, "I can offer one hundred thousand and maybe he will agree to two."

Chauncey made eye contact with Billy and quietly puts up two fingers. Billy saw the fingers and nodded his head in the affirmative. Chauncey instructed Clinton, "Do it. Two hundred thousand dollars -- close the deal."

The sign on the wall read "JP Morgan, and Company". The lavish reception area was filled with the finest antiques. Two male clerks sat at desks in front of a door leading to the head office. The main entrance was at the other end of the room. This door opened. Billy, Chauncey, Cornelius II, Willie, several lawyers, and several Vanderbilt Pinkertons entered. The last to enter was Henry Simon, the personal valet to King Billy, who would years later become the head butler at the Breakers in Newport. As the men walked through the reception area, the two clerks stood and the doors to the head office opened. Out walked a youthful JP Morgan.

After the "hellos" and an exchange of pleasantries, other various greetings they all followed JP into his office suite. If the lobby was first class, JP's office was fit for a king or a prime minister – a role into which he was about to be molded. On one side was a large conference table; the other was filled with sofas, chairs, tables, a bar, and JP's grand mahogany desk.

As everyone settled into their seats, JP began: "So King Billy, the richest person on the planet and the most powerful man in America. How can I help you?"

"Now that the trial is finished, we are interested in selling a small amount of stock in the Central."

"How much?"

"At the right price, our brilliant treasurer, Prince Cornelius here, calculates that if we were to receive between $120 and $130 per share, we could net $35,000,000 and still retain 80% of the company."

JP informed him, "To get that price we may need to bring in some people your father wouldn't like."

Chauncey asked, "Like whom?"

Mr. Morgan answered, "William Astor, for one."

King Billy demanded, "If you think I would give that son of a bitch a piece of my company…"

Chauncey interrupted, "Billy, maybe we should look at this as an opportunity?"

"What opportunity?"

"Well, for one thing, the Astors and the Vanderbilts wouldn't be bitter enemies anymore. You would be linked together, aligned in business, and considering our other mutual enterprises this may be a novel idea."

Cornelius offered a clarification, "So long as we aren't linked through marriage."

JP continued, "Astor is only demanding one seat on the New York Central Board. Don't deny yourself just because there is a rivalry between the two families."

Billy, "It's not just the two families but the Houses and those in their Courts and their subjects could rise up in protest."

JP continued, "Take the thirty five million and invest it into government bonds. This worked very well a decade ago so why not do it again? It will guarantee a never ending fortune, a heredity line that will reign for a thousand years."

Billy disagreed, "While you may believe that our US bonds turned into a wise investment, the profits were barely able to be monetized. For the first time in this nation's history the government began deficit spending to pay for the war."

Chauncey, "During the war we invested $400 million and without imposing a national tax simply printing money will devalue those government bonds that we all now own."

JP, "These families were all compensated for forgiving those bonds."

Billy, "Yes JP, but those secondary benefits will never fully be enjoyed by our families if they cannot be recognized or for that matter ever known outside of the White House and of those at Court for fear of an uprising."

Chauncey added, "The public has already been growing opposed to the control of such great property by a single man or a single family. They already believe we rule by might."

JP, "By right you certainly have control of property."

Billy, "No matter, this public feeling still exists."

While the wealth and power of King Billy and the House of Vanderbilt continued to grow, Billy's brother Corneel had been summoned to meet with his attorney, Scott Lord, at his office.

"I must say, Corneel, this year-long trip is probably not what you should be doing."

"I just need to clear my head and get out of the city."

"You can't afford it. You have $600,000 sitting in trust and another $200,000 in cash and that doesn't account for my $5,000 fee. You spend nearly ten thousand a year and that doesn't include your gambling and ongoing living expenses. Now you tell me about a house you're buying in Hartford for $50,000 and a trip that sounds like it will cost another fifty."

"I can always borrow some money if I need to, or ask one of my nephews."

"Have you learned nothing from all this litigation?" Mr. Lord asked in disbelief and then facetiously added, "Corneel, if you could afford it, I could drop all my other clients and represent you full time."

Only a few days later Corneel was sitting in a fancy backroom casino playing cards with three gentlemen. The bets were high – thousands of dollars in some of the large pots, and Corneel was losing money quickly. One waitress brought Corneel a drink and placed it in front of him, removing the three empty glasses. A second waitress brought over a small plate with cocaine on it. Like a lewd drunken fool he did a line, and then quickly did another.

Corneel, I think you should call it a night," said one of the gamblers.

"I'm fine."

"I'm about to raise you. You can't afford this hand. There's already fifty thousand in the pot."

Corneel sniffed another line of cocaine, threw back his drink and said, "Call or raise, either way you can't beat my hand."

The other gambler said, "That's definitely the words of a bluffer."

"All right Corneel, I've already got $10,000 of yours, but I'll force that $5,000 in chips in front of you into the pot. This is your last warning."

Corneel looked at his hand. He was holding three Aces and two Kings – Full House. "I'll be happy to take another $5,000 from you."

"I warned you. Raise five thousand."

The Gambler pushed in his chips. He looked at his cards. Three twos and One Ace – the fifth card was hidden behind the others, but it looked like Corneel was going to win a $60,000 pot. Corneel pushed in his last chips and called the hand.

The second gambler said, "Okay, boys who's going home rich and who just lost all their money? Corneel, it's the moment of truth."

Corneel turned over his full house. The Gambler revealed his three twos and then the Ace as Corneel jumped in joy, "Yes."

The Gambler continued, "Sorry Corneel, no hard feelings" as he turned over his final card. Another two – four of a kind, the winning hand.

Corneel was shocked. The Gambler called over the two security guards to come and remove Corneel. He said, "I'm sorry Corneel, but you're broke and you owe everyone at this table money that you don't have. It's time for you to leave."

Corneel was escorted out begging to borrow more money. Outside he found himself beneath a street sign that read "Fifth Avenue," facing north up Manhattan. In the distance were thousands of ironworkers, artisans, craftsman, steel fixers, painters, carpenters, pipefitters, and endless day laborers erecting the Vanderbilt palaces of his brother's family.

Dawn was just beginning to break. Corneel was drunk and high on cocaine. He was talking to himself and grinding his teeth as he crossed the street. He entered the Glenham Hotel and walked through the lobby which was empty except for a few bellmen and two maids cleaning from the night before. A manager saw Corneel and approached him, "Mr. Vanderbilt, how are you, sir?"

He could not stop mumbling to himself, "He had one ace, one ace, I had three, two kings, he must have cheated. Won with twos, all the twos, must have cheated, I can sue."

"Sir."

Barely able to speak clearly, Corneal admitted, "I need some cash, let me write you a check."

The manager was not amused, "Sir, I need to inform you that your last check for five hundred dollars was not honored by the bank. The hotel needs to be paid in cash – today."

Corneel responded, "I'll go to the bank later, just give me fifty dollars now and I'll pay it all back later."

"I can't do that, sir. This hotel can no longer extend credit to you Mr. Vanderbilt."

Screaming, "I am a Vanderbilt. You will give me the money," Corneel grabbed the manager by his coat. "You listen to me, you're conspiring against me too. You gave him the fourth two. You did, didn't you! It was you!" Several bellmen came rushing to separate Corneel and the manager. While they restrained Corneel like a common thief, the manager informed him, "Mr. Vanderbilt, you are no longer welcome at this hotel. Gentlemen, escort Mr. Vanderbilt to his room, put him to bed, and in the morning we will have him arrested for writing fraudulent checks."

The footmen escorted Corneel to his room and slammed the door shut after him. Corneel fell to the floor in tremendous defeat. He slowly picked himself up and walked toward his desk. He sat at his desk and opened the top drawer. In it was a .38 caliber Smith. He picked up the gun, put it in his mouth and pulled the trigger.

Cornelius Jeremiah Vanderbilt, son of the Commodore, committed suicide at the age of fifty-one. He had no fortune to leave behind. In fact, every dollar he had inherited from the Commodore was gone. In Hartford alone he left debts of $15,000. The house he had purchased for $50,000 was left to cover outstanding debts. Eventually it was sold at auction, the highest bid being only $15,000.

The first namesake of Commodore Vanderbilt died a broken man – broken financially and broken in life. He was the Wicked Son.

The Court of Newport

What we want
cannot come fast enough
What we don't want
is here tomorrow

You had been given a great gift. Your nerves were on edge. There were but a few moments before your life would change forever, though whether for better or for worse, you did not know. The excitement of the moment was overpowering, and provided an inner strength which soon replaced your anxiety with courage. You were perfectly qualified, properly trained and your employment interview had gone very well, considering you were only eighteen years of age. Your outward appearance was flawless—your uniform, your hair, your nails, your shoes, all appeared perfect. This outward appearance of the ideal novice maid stood in opposition to your intellect and passion for reading the great works of the day. Had the household been aware of these predilections, you would have been ostracized, without question. All this for a job that pays less than fifteen cents per day! A deep breath, a moment to smile, and one last glance out over the Cliff Walk, listening to the ocean crashing below. It's time. It's your debut. You are about to make your own debut at Gertrude Vanderbilt's Coming Out Party.

In your chambermaid uniform you race across the lawn and through the gardens to Mama's summer palace known to all as Mrs. Vanderbilt's 'Breakers Mansion'. You didn't want to be late, so entered through the servants' hall into the pantry and its adjoining kitchen.

"What the devil are you doing? We only have one hour! Some of you will lose your jobs tonight if this party is not perfect." Madame Du Vain, the middle-aged housekeeper was trying in vain to assemble the servants under her charge. Nothing was working. Running in circles like painted horses on a merry-go-round, but going nowhere, were cooks, kitchen maids, chambermaids, footmen, coachmen, and valets. Even Charlie, the grandfatherly Negro bald-headed gardener, who couldn't have been younger than eighty, was peeling carrots, amused by the comedy playing out before him – a *comedy of errors* which he had enjoyed a front row seat many times during his years of service.

A young chambermaid dressed in a black uniform and white apron and bonnet asked in a soothing voice, "Can I help you?"

"I'm looking for Madam Du Vain."

"She's the frenzied one. My name is Trudy."

"I'm Victoria."

"Oh, you're the new girl. Take these," as she handed over a tray of dishes.

"You picked some night to begin your employment. Okay, follow me."

"What's happening?

"Tonight is Gertrude Vanderbilt's coming out party."

Like a great ballet or the *Pops of Boston* popping, cooks were chopping, chefs were cooking, maids were running here and there, fart catchers were chasing the Page Boys, who in turn were chasing the young maids, and the valets were discombobulated. Madame Du Vain was the conductor, yelling and twirling her baton to reach a crescendo. The head chef, who had only been with the Vanderbilts for two weeks, looked shocked, threw down his towel, and left the kitchen in exasperation. All of these antics amused only an audience of one, old faithful, Charlie. This was one of the best comic operas he had witnessed. All debutante balls resulted in extraordinary mayhem, and this was to be the most elaborate of all, <u>the</u> social event of the Newport summer of 1895.

Suddenly came the encore—a loud crash! The head chef ran back into the kitchen followed by several footmen. In a pure Parisian French and carrying significant weight, not just vocally, "Madame du Vain, S'il vous plait! Guardez vous! Ne laissez pas tomber les desserts."

A footman spoke up, "Chef, Madame Du Vain does not speak French."

"Madam—pleez—tell your ouvriers to finish flooring my dessertz.!" The chef stormed out as the mess was quickly cleaned up. As Du Vain looked around, everyone began hustling about again. She sighed, hoping that the worst was over, turned, and then looked and stared in bewilderment directly at you..

Angrily she asked, "*Who* are you?"

"This is Victoria. She's the new girl," Trudy explained.

Victoria curtsied.

"Listen to Trudy here. Do what she does and go where she goes and do not, under any circumstances, talk to anybody. Especially me!"

A chambermaid approached Du Vain, "Madame, Mrs. Vanderbilt's maid just called down. Apparently Mrs. Vanderbilt is raving mad and wants to see you immediately."

Snapping her fingers, "You two come with me."

You and Trudy followed Du Vain, hoping that she wouldn't turn around again and resume shouting. You moved from the servant's area through the morning room and entered the grand hall.

Like a peninsula, the Breakers was surrounded on three sides by roads that were most often closed when the family was in residence. On the east side, across the manicured lawns was a reef. The sound of the Atlantic Ocean breaking onto the rocks was how the Breakers had received its name. Although sitting on thirteen acres, the mansion itself consumed only an acre and its rooms were aligned symmetrically around a great hall two stories high. This ornately galleried hall was paved in marble and surrounded by walls of Caen stone, alabaster and marble columns which were decorated with frieze, cornice, and entablature. It was like living inside a piece of royal jewelry.

As you passed through the hall, your eyes were drawn to the brilliant wall of glass French doors which opened onto the loggia and through which, beyond the green grass and the blue water, you could see the remains of the orange sun setting in the western sky. On one side of the great hall were several vestibules leading to the main entrance. On the other side were the library, music room, and morning room. At one end was a grand staircase rising to a landing from which twin flights curved upwards to the second floor galleria. The entire house was adorned further with an abundance of footmen, many of whom seemed to have no role other than standing at attention guarding a wall or a plant or even nothing at all.

Tonight, except for the dining room located behind the grand staircase, the rooms on the main floor were bare of furniture. The orchestra was fine tuning their instruments while servants sought perfection to every detail of food, wine, champagne, flowers, before the thousands of guests would arrive at midnight. You had been trained never to use the grand staircase, instead to travel only by those passages and stairs reserved for the invisible servants—that the family should never feel as if you are intruding upon their home.

Walking through the halls with Du Vain, Trudy elaborated on some of the laws of the household: "Here at the Breakers, it is most important to always remember your place. There is a hierarchy amongst the royals. Do not speak to anyone above you. Anyone below you is permitted. The House Guards and the Pinkertons...well, just keep away from them. Because we are in Newport Castle and not in the city, footmen are considered above us. They only answer to Mrs. Vanderbilt's lady's maid, the valets, the head chef, Madam Du Vain and the butler, Mr. Simon. Under no circumstances shall you speak with anyone in the family or any other gentleman or lady unless they speak to you first. Remember your place and you will do just fine. Your training at Marble House will be helpful, but this is not any mansion; this is a royal court."

TRAINING: Since you were fourteen, you have been trained in domestic service, but it seemed as long ago as you could remember. You began your official employment and training as a scullery maid, although since turning twelve, you assisted the seamstresses. A scullery maid was absolutely the worst job. As the lowest ranked and youngest of the female servants, you were an assistant to a junior kitchen maid. One might think that the cleaning and scouring in the kitchen was the worst part of your job, but what you hated most was the plucking of fowl and the scaling of fish. You were not allowed to eat with the other household servants but as a privilege you were sometimes allowed to serve them. By fifteen, you were fortunate to be promoted to laundry maid; the best part of that job was that you didn't smell like fish and meat all day long. You would wash, dry, fold or iron every piece of clothing, towel, bedlinen, tablecloth and napkin used by the family and all the servants. At sixteen, you were finally allowed upstairs, where you entered a world you had not even imagined in your fantasies. As an "upstairs maid," you started as a chambermaid responsible for maintaining the family's bedrooms and keeping the fireplaces lit. At seventeen you became a parlor maid, cleaning reception and living areas and serving afternoon tea. Finally, last year you were promoted to housemaid, reporting to the head housemaid, who reported to the housekeeper, who reported to the butler, who reported to the lady of the house. However, when you entered service at the Breakers, you had to return to serving as a chambermaid.

Mrs. Vanderbilt's bedroom was, not surprisingly, the largest in the Breakers, and the only one not incorporating any ninety degree corners. It was bright in its floral design and the pink furniture seemed actually to evoke the aroma of roses. The entire apartment was comprised of a bedroom, dressing room, sitting room, bathrooms and closets, each of which was twice the size of the bedroom you shared with two other maids.

Mrs. Vanderbilt was at her desk, reading letters that her person maid, Anne, had organized in order of priority, while keeping the envelopes away from Mrs. Vanderbilt's eyes. Du Vain knocked from the corridor.

Mrs. Vanderbilt's commanding voice, "Come." As the three of you entered, Mrs. Vanderbilt put Du Vain on the defensive, "*What* is this?" She handed a note to Anne who passed it along to Du Vain, but before she could read the first sentence, Mrs. Vanderbilt could not contain her irritation for one moment longer. "This is why Gertrude is not to be left to her own. She is a child and requires constant supervision. In the Lord's name, how was an invitation sent to Consuelo? You know of my relationship with her mother. Not one foot.

That is the policy in my home. Alva is not to step one foot in this house."

Mama's apartment connected to Papa's suite which unlike most European palaces was much smaller compared to that of a queens' chambers. As King Cornelius entered, Mrs. Vanderbilt brought the Gertrude matter to his attention. "Have you seen this?"

"Seen what?

"Who gave Gertrude permission to invite anyone? It may be her coming out party but it is my ball. It is my house."

"Whom did she invite?"

"Consuelo."

"Well she's sweet and she's your niece."

"I have no problem with her, but, Du Vain, I presume that Alva has been invited as well?"

"Yes, she and Miss Consuelo both responded in the affirmative."

Calming the situation, the King offered, "Alice, my dear, with a thousand people coming tonight, you will hardly notice her."

Realizing her grave mistake and utterly embarrassed, Du Vain was forced to clarify, "Begging your pardon, but according to the dinner's seating plan, both Mrs. Vanderbilt and Consuelo…"

Mrs. Vanderbilt swiftly interjected, "Do not ever call her that— and certainly not in my presence. She is nothing more than a blind monkey drinking holy water…"

Du Vain, "It was a slip of the tongue and I apologize, but downstairs we always refer to her…"

"Shut your yap. Do not interrupt me."

Du Vain was silent while Trudy stood behind her doing everything she could to hide any and every part of her mouth so as not to appear to be cracking a little smile. It wasn't just Du Vain. Every housekeeper at court was resented by the rest of the staff. If any of them had revealed even the slightest empathy they would have been fired for not being evil enough. Even the others at Newport Castle feared Du Vain, but ironically no one was more terrified than Du Vain, for when Mama spoke to her, it was as if a dagger was thrust into her chest, even if the words themselves were pleasant. Alva however, unmasked Mama and her words were filled with vitriol. "In this house, you and everyone else will call her Alva. Or if you prefer, you can call her Mrs. Vanderbilt number two or junior or the lesser."

Du Vain realized that Mrs. Vanderbilt had attempted to lighten the mood, so she chuckled. Mrs. Vanderbilt continued, "Gertrude will absolutely be punished for this. As a young lady she cannot make decisions for herself, particularly on matters like acquaintances and callers. What, is she going to marry whomever she wants? We cannot have her believing she is in control of her life, especially once she has come out. Society may mistake us for the Wilsons."

The King approached his wife, "Well what's done is done. We cannot un-invite them."

"Of course we can."

"We mustn't."

After a thought, "Very well then," she pointed to Du Vain to leave. "You may go."

Before leaving the room Du Vain asked, "Mrs. Vanderbilt, next to whom at the table shall I sit Mrs...van...der...Alva?

"Well don't put her next to me. As far as I am concerned, she can dine with the scullery maids."

King Cornelius laughed and sat on the sofa as you, Trudy, and Du Vain left the bedroom. With the two of them finally alone, Mrs. Vanderbilt rose from her seat and walked to the window to peek through the drapes at the throng of people descending on the Breakers. The main gate was thirty feet high and crafted of wrought iron. On top of the gateway was the elaborate scrollwork including the oak leaf family crest surrounding the initials of Cornelius Vanderbilt, "*CV.*" Single gates providing access to the sidewalks flanked the main gates. There were two main gateways, the main entrance on Ochre Point Avenue and the main exit on Sheppard Avenue. These two gateways were part of a twelve-foot-high Genoese-style limestone and iron fence that bordered the property on all sides but that of the Atlantic Ocean. Encircling the entrance were four bronze lamp posts decorated with molded figures that were mounted on three-foot limestone pedestals with bronze standards standing high with four globes on each. A gravel path led from the main gate to a large porte-cochere. Standing throughout the grounds were footmen and House Guards decorated in court livery and white silk stockings that brightened the lawns and gardens and which contrasted with the stately grey of the mansion. Ostentatiously dressed, they were also positioned alongside the outer fences along all three avenues. Police and Pinkertons were trying their best to keep the crowds back while giving reporters appropriate access but at the same time keeping the streets closed as guests in horse drawn carriages approached the Breakers. Excess also visible, as each carriage was flanked by two footmen in front and two in back, dressed in their respective families' formal court livery.

Mrs. Vanderbilt was pleased that events outside were proceeding according to her plan. She returned to her desk and resumed reading her correspondence. "Cornelius, perhaps it's good for Alva to pay us a visit. Let her and Caroline Astor both dine at the Breakers. Let the experience overwhelm them so we can enjoy their astonishment as they realize, once again, that we have surpassed them both in grandeur and in style."

"This rivalry between you and Alva must one day come to an end before someone is irreparably blemished," replied Cornelius. This reply startled Mrs. Vanderbilt as she expected and required unquestioned loyalty and obedience from her husband. "I agree though, that she is not ladylike. Her position as a mistress would have prevented her from entering society had she not taken up with your brother. Willie is such a fool. I knew from the moment he married Alva that she would be a constant hindrance. What do you expect from an abolitionist? She is akin to Caroline Astor, but no matter how hard she tries, Alva can never attain the status of a Mrs. Astor. And Caroline is merely an Astor and nothing more – a family of hugger-muggers and head of a secondary Court."

The King rose from the sofa and headed toward the door as Mrs. Vanderbilt continued, "The scuttlebutt in Newport is that Oliver Belmont will be hosting a ball for the Duke before the end of the summer. To which I have been saying, 'nothing like having your new husband pay for your daughter's ball'."

"That's if the Duke ever gets here."

Mrs. Vanderbilt, "Leave it to Alva - she'll make sure the Duke arrives. I'm sure she's already received the consent of Queen Victoria."

"Must we find a European royal to marry Gertrude," King Cornelius asked?

"Of course not. For as much as I detest Alva, I have a soft spot for Consuelo. I feel sadness for her. She is being forced into a loveless marriage. Her husband has been chosen for her. Gertrude, on the other hand, will be able to choose from a group of appropriate suitors. No, it is Neily about whose future I am deeply worried."

"He will marry soon."

Mrs. Vanderbilt looked into his eyes in earnest, "Cornelius, just remember that the Breakers isn't simply a mansion. It's a palace, a symbol of the head of the House of Vanderbilt. If Consuelo becomes engaged to the Duke, it will put enormous pressure on Neily to marry a fitting girl and produce a male heir. The head of the fourth generation of Vanderbilts must descend from our side of the family and not from Alva's."

"Well I leave it in your good hands. It seems as if some of our dinner guests are arriving. I will see you downstairs."

Outside the main entrance under the porte-cochere, the first carriage to arrive was Willie Vanderbilt, a Duke at Court, Cornelius' brother, and Alva's ex-husband. Footmen opened the door and Willie was greeted by the butler, Simon, and King Cornelius' valet, Mr. Addison. As Willie stepped out, he acknowledged Simon, "good to see you as always."

"Thank you Mr. Vanderbilt. Your brother awaits you in the library. Mr. Addison will escort you."

Willie and Mr. Addison entered the Breakers as the doormen opened the two outer wrought iron doors. Entering a small enclosed courtyard they took several steps and walked through two oak carved doors fit for giants which two footmen had struggled to open from the inside. As music, soft yet elegant, could be heard, they entered the foyer and continued into the vestibule. As they passed by Trudy, she stood aside, bowed her head, and after they passed she continued to the porte-cochere. The butler was already greeting the next guests, Mr. Richard Morris Hunt and his daughter, twenty year old Esther Hunt.

"Mr. Hunt, welcome back to the house that you built"

"You are too kind Simon, but it was your employer who built it. I merely designed it."

As the pleasantries continued, Trudy inconspicuously moved toward Esther who secretly handed her a note, "this is for Gertrude."

Upstairs, an inspection was taking place in Mrs. Vanderbilt's bedroom. Anne, Mrs. Vanderbilt's lady's maid, was showcasing the hair and garments of her youngest children, nine year old Gladys and fifteen year old Reggie. Reggie was arguing, "Mother, I think you are being unreasonable. She is a nice girl from a good family."

"Her family is Catholic," countered Mrs. Vanderbilt.

"So what of it?"

"And you were seen drinking with her"

"I wasn't drunk."

"Ah, so I should be pleased that I have a fifteen year old son who is an inebriant drinking with a Catholic girl who is four years older than he."

"How shallow can you possibly be?"

"Anne, do you see the conduct I have to deal with here?"

Reggie was frustrated, "Sending me off to school at St. George's this fall is not going to change anything. You think they don't drink there?"

"I'm sure they do, but at least you won't be canoodling with second class girls."

"I'm almost sixteen. There are girls my age downstairs who are having babies."

"Don't you speak like that in front of your sister. Not in this house. This is a house of the Lord."

Gladys perks up, "It's okay Mama, I already know. Betty is going to have a baby."

Mrs. Vanderbilt focused her attention back to Anne, "Who is Betty."

"She use to work downstairs, but Du Vain is bringing her upstairs as a nursemaid."

"Not anymore. Tell Du Vain that she is to be relieved immediately."

"Shall I tell her to hire out for a replacement?"

"No, tell her to find someone already here."

– Gertrude's Bedroom –

"Yes," I responded to a knock at my door as Victoria, you assisted me with my jewelry. Trudy walked in, handed me a note and said, "Miss Hunt asked me to give this to you."

"Thank you Trudy."

I opened the small letter:

My dearest Gertrude.

To see her is to love her, and love her forever. For nature made her what she is, and never made another.

With all my heart,
Esther.

My heart was pounding and I smiled and hugged the letter to my chest so my soul could feel Esther. Another knock at the door, "Enter."

Du Vain entered and said to me, "Excuse me Lady Gertrude. I need to speak with Trudy and Victoria."

Paying almost no attention to Du Vain, I responded, "You can say whatever you must in my presence. I need their help and I don't want to be even one minute late."

"Very good," she turned to Trudy and Victoria, "Pay attention girls, Mrs. Vanderbilt has ordered that I terminate Betty, and I've decided that for the summer season you Victoria, will be the new nursemaid. Gladys is nine and Reggie is fifteen. You are responsible for both of them while they are in residence at the Breakers. Everything from schedule, to escorting them to social functions, planning their attire, keeping them entertained, and seeing to their educational needs. The family prays in the Royal Chapel every day, and Reggie is often late – make sure he's not and make sure he doesn't drink."

Du Vain did not wait around for questions. Trudy was definitely relieved as Reggie didn't much care for her and on occasion would drive her zany. Their relationship was strained at best. Victoria, the look on your face was priceless. Since sunset you had been demoted from housemaid to chambermaid, and now you had been designated the new nursemaid to a fifteen year old alcoholic, a troublesome condition which would ultimately lead to his premature death.

Except for the invitations to Alva and her daughter Consuelo, each of the thousand guests who were to arrive at midnight had been carefully evaluated, securitized, and analyzed for their status in society and their position in business. Food was to be served, but only a select few were invited for the dinner. Not even I was so naïve as to believe that this event was for my benefit. If it were my choice, I would never 'come out', but as I approached twenty years of age, it was better for my parents to host an aide ball than to feel the rumors gaining strength. How could my wardrobe or jewels fuel competing newspapers and journals to write about something so insignificant? So there they were, all twenty or so of them, downstairs, waiting for my grand entrance. As the eldest daughter, Papa was the most excited; he was proud of his eldest daughter and for that I could smile for him. Finally it was his turn.

Who doesn't enjoy the combination of business and pleasure? It was not like decisions made or circumstances experienced in your world Victoria, the real world – a world which I forever longed for, even if in it I were to fail. To eat bread with cheese or jam, to visit the pub for a beer or to be intoxicated with cheap whiskey, to immerse yourself in the latest romance novel or follow society's gossip in the daily paper, rather than be the subject of it... I presume the grandest decision you will make, that of whom to marry, it will be your decision alone. An heiress is not permitted to make such decisions. Her job is to play a role. For the first part of her life, the role is defined by her mother and for the second part of her life, the script is written by her husband. What to think and say, whom to call upon, where to go, and how to live. "Why" is not in the vocabulary of an heiress. If you are not allowed to make decisions, there is simply no reason to ask why. To question is the prerogative of men whether the commoners in the square, or the barons in the library downstairs.

Experiences, questions, decisions – my role has been rehearsed, the three acts have been written and the outcomes' effects will last forever and must stand the test of time. The test is not a path I pursue for a wrong turn can jeopardize my pre-determined fate. Experiences, questions, decisions – the barons role has not been rehearsed, the scripts have not been written, though the effects will also last forever and must survive the same timely test. The baron understands that no business, like societies, can ever stand the test of time for that is the great mythology in business and society. Are the farms in America closing because people are no longer eating, or has the 'every man for himself' capitalist mentality allowed corruption and price fixing, causing prices to rise, demand to fall, and workers who can never earn a living wage? Will the European colonies continue to fall in Africa, India, and the Orient, or is the worst over for them? The greatest example is Julius Caesar's two millennia Roman Empire, but the list goes on: the Pharaohs in Egypt, Genghis Kahn and the savage Mongols, the four hundred year reign in China of the Han Dynasty, the thousand years of the Byzantines in the Near East, the three continent empire of the Persians, and most recently, the Holy Roman Empire which fell to Napoleon, which would have never taken place without the French Revolution in the previous century. A revolution inspired by the American Revolutionaries, ironically aided by the French monarchy which finally fell to the mobs at Marie Antoinette's Versailles. Where will America be in the last century of this millennium? A great power, a defeated people, or in the middle of another 100 years war?

Many societies once great, indestructible and infinite are now just a passage read in a classical text. History in its simplest form is physics, for everything that goes up must come down. The caution for the heiress and the baron is that the slower things go up, the slower they fall and conversely the faster one rises, oh how quick he shall fall. Papa and Uncle Willie understood this, for they were mentored well –

all of them having learned from both the strength of the Commodore and the struggle to improve upon his weaknesses.

While guests mingled in the grand hall feasting on champagne and delicacies as the orchestra played, battle plans were being drawn in the library by three men: Papa Cornelius Vanderbilt, Uncle Willie Vanderbilt, and Chauncey Depew.

Chauncey explained the situation, "The Astors are again threatening to compete directly against the Vanderbilt rail lines. If we want to penetrate the mid-west it makes more sense to buy out the Astors than build competing rail lines. In fact, I believe we have no choice. If we learned anything from the Nickel Plate and the South Pennsylvania Railroad incidents, it is that if we compete with the Astors, we do so at great risk."

"I agree." Willie concurred, "Going head to head with them could be very expensive, especially if we force them into another price war."

Cornelius added, "Our New York Central is the most efficient train system in the world. Two points to remember Chauncey. Why would we acquire a shabby railroad? And if we do, let's make sure there's no Daniel Drew or Jay Gould behind Astor, watering the deal."

BANG BANG BANG

– Flashback –

BANG BANG BANG

The Chairman, an elderly man, bangs his gavel. The legislature hearing room in Albany overflows with spectators, journalists, lawyers, and some of the wealthiest people of the day. The Commodore himself, commanding and very tall with a colt's tooth, enters flanked by his legal and security entourage lead by a younger, perhaps sharper in his youth, Chauncey Depew. His arch enemy, William Backhouse Astor Jr., the forty year old husband of society's queen, Mrs. Astor, enters next, followed by the Commodore's oldest and greatest rival, seventy year old Daniel Drew, and his two much younger protégés, Jay Gould and Jim Fisk.

By 1870, America had fought a vicious Civil War and the Industrial Revolution was ever more influential in the lives of Americans from all walks of life. The expanding United States would be ruled by coal and steel, lugged across the country by railroad. The House of Vanderbilt and the House of Astor would fight to the bitter end for control of the US railroad industry. And time and time again one house would prevail.

BANG BANG BANG. State Attorney Brown, representing the committee, sits next to the Chairman who is a typical white haired, foul mouthed, fifty cigarettes a day, yearning to be rich, New York politician about whom there is nothing charming. Attorney Brown can no longer hide his frustration, "Mr. Drew can you please tell this committee what the term 'watered stock' means."

"Again, I say I'm not familiar with that term." The Commodore glances at Drew, shaking his head in disbelief.

"Are they not going to ask Astor about his involvement?" whispered the Commodore to Chauncey."

"Looks like they are throwing Drew to the lions."

Attorney Brown continues questioning Daniel Drew, "Can you tell this committee and the press and the general public who have joined us here today what the term 'selling stock short' means?"

"Yes, it simply means rather than betting on a stock price going higher, it means betting that the stock will go lower."

"And how exactly does this work?"

"It's very simple." Drew explains, "An investor borrows shares and immediately sells them. Then, after the stock price falls, the investor uses the money from the sale to buy back the shares at a lower price, returns the borrowed shares, and keeps the difference as a profit."

"In this type of transaction, what happens to the investor if rather than the stock price going down, it goes up?"

"In that case, the investor would be forced to use his own funds to cover the shortfall. The higher the stock price, the more the investor must spend to buy back the number of shares he borrowed. One could easily lose a great sum of money."

Again the Commodore whispers to Chauncey, "You don't just lose your money. The son of a bitch is left with no assets. It's like burning your money"

Drew hopes that the attorney is finished with this line of questioning, but even he realizes where the questions are leading, so he offers, "Mr. Brown, I really am not familiar with the term: 'watered stock'."

"So under oath before this committee and God, understanding the penalties of perjury, and to be absolutely clear, you have never heard of, nor used in any context whatsoever, the term 'watered stock'?" As the tone of the questioning becomes more heated, the Commodore glowers at Daniel Drew and William Astor. As soon as Astor is eye to eye with the Vanderbilt patriarch, the Commodore smiles narcissistically. Astor's bleeding wound was soon to feel the sting as if a finely peeled juicy onion were rubbed on it.

"That is the absolute truth."

"Very well then Mr. Drew." Attorney Brown continues, "I have given you three opportunities. I don't suppose your co-conspirators will answer?"

The Astor attorney rises in opposition, "Mr. Chairman, I object to Mr. Brown alleging that there is any conspiracy between my client, Mr. Astor and Messrs. Drew, Gould and Fisk."

The Chairman responds, "Counselor, this is not a criminal proceeding. There's nothing here for you to object to. Proceed Mr. Brown."

"Mr. Vanderbilt, would you be so kind as to define for this committee what the term 'watered stock' means?"

Almost gleefully, in an unusually respectful manner the Commodore answers the question, "Yuh, it's spreading information about a stock and then it goes up. But they lie, they're all liars I say. So the price goes up and they knew the information was bullshit and if the public knew it too the price would fall."

Brown continues, "Mr. Drew, does that sound familiar to you?"

"No, never, and to use such language!"

Brown ignores Drew's editorial comment and turns back to the Commodore, "Mr. Vanderbilt, do you know the origin of the term 'watered stock'?"

"Cattle sellers would force their cattle to drink a lot of water which would increase the weight of the cattle. Naturally, the weight would go down once the cow pissed." The tension of the hearing is finally broken as everyone in the chamber gets a much needed chuckle from the Commodore's choice of words.

Chauncey offers a suggestion to the Commodore, "Sir, the preferred word is 'urinate'."

"Shit Chauncey, what you say?"

The laughing continues as the Chairman bangs his gavel for order. "Order, order. Mr. Vanderbilt please, this is a public hearing." Yet, the Commodore loves the attention.

With his smoky breath he quietly tells Chauncey, "It's not enough that the committee sees Drew and Astor for the crooked liars they are. I win when the committee realizes that the people are on my side."

Brown continues, "Mr. Vanderbilt, do you know who coined the phrase 'watered stock'?"

"Well it was Mr. Drew, from his days as a cattle seller." Not only did Drew deny knowing the phrase but again the audience's laughter cannot be controlled as everyone realizes the irony that it was Drew himself who came up with the term.

"Mr. Vanderbilt, isn't it true that on at least three occasions, Daniel Drew watered the stock of various railroad companies in which you were buying stock, and then tried to sell the stock short?"

"He did, that pig."

"Was he successful?"

"Not even once, I say."

"In fact, in each instance you were purchasing more stock than they were selling, and driving the price up. Isn't that true?"

"They're stupid thieves. They walked right into my ambush."

"Can you explain how and when these events transpired, and who was involved?"

Chauncey whispers into the Commodore's ear, "Don't worry. The Chairman won't allow that question to be answered. He'll protect Astor."

A senator interrupts the proceedings, "Mr. Chairman, before we pursue this line of questioning, perhaps this is a good time for the committee to adjourn for the day."

"I agree. Is there a motion to adjourn?"

"So moved."

"Is there a second?"

"Second!"

To conclude the rules of the chamber in bringing the meeting to a close, he asks, "Any objections?"

The crowd erupts in disapproval, shouting, "No! We want the truth! Represent the people! Regulate the railroads! We won't drink bilge water! We want clean cars! Get the odors out of the trains! Boooo!"

The Chairman bangs his gavel, "Order. Order. The motion is carried. We are adjourned for the day." As the senators on the dais are silent the Chairman bangs the gavel. BANG. BANG. BANG.

Although since Biblical times the world has rotated on its axis at exactly the same speed as it does today, each generation in each century in each millennia can sense that time, for them, is moving more quickly than for their predecessors. Perhaps it is simply that through innovation and new technologies, what once took a week now takes only a day, and in one hundred years it may take only an hour, and then a minute, and eventually a second, or a fraction of second and so on. The first explorers to the Americas sailed for more than two months, while today one can complete this voyage comfortably in ten days. A letter which one hundred years ago was carried by wagon from New York to Chicago now takes less than thirty-five hours by train.

In each generation, the innovators are driven not just by excellence but also by speed. The time it takes to cook a meal, heat a building, mine for coal, construct a building and almost everything we see and touch benefits from these visionaries. Such men are businessmen, industrialists, and entrepreneurs – men like William Astor and my great grandfather. Acceleration in time however was not an ally of the Astor's real estate fortune. A month's rental income increases slowly, unlike the Commodore's shipping and railroad industries which can take advantage of innovation. Papa would constantly preach that business was about two things, 'time and money', and that decreasing travel time through innovation, expanding routes, or eliminating competition resulted in more trips carrying more passengers and freight and therefore greater profits for the House of Vanderbilt.

Rapid economic expansion comes with risks. The banks were fueling this new exuberance, and in the absence of any regulations they were lending money recklessly just to remain competitive. As a result, between 1812 and 1870 the United States had experienced twelve recessions and two depressions. The first depression followed the War of 1812 when bank notes quickly depreciated as a result of post war inflation; for six years there were widespread foreclosures resulting in significant bank failures and collapsing real estate prices, while the only metric in the market rising was unemployment. The second led to the worldwide panic of 1857 when the Ohio Life Insurance and Trust Company failed due to plummeting agricultural exports to Europe following the Crimean War. The result was a bursting of the American railroad bubble, runs on banks worldwide, and over five thousand businesses forced to close their doors.

The Commodore and his son, my grandfather, William Henry ("Billy") Vanderbilt, would sell when everyone else was in a purchasing euphoria, and when many shareholders were dumping stocks, the Vanderbilts were buyers. They were simply buying low and selling high. Physics dictate that whatever goes up must come down. As such once all the buyers are invested in the stock market with no one left to bid the seller's prices determine the strike price and therefore the cost of everything must fall. Likewise, once all the sellers and 'the shorts' are out of the market, the buyers dictate the prices forcing them to rise. The pendulum dictates that if buyers outnumber sellers prices rise and if sellers outnumber buyers prices fall. It has been that way for all of history in every asset class whether selling financial securities or coffee and it will forever continue because it is scientific truth – it is physics.

Frustration and concern were an understatement of their mood as William Astor, Daniel Drew, Jay Gould and Jim Fisk panicked in 1870 Albany as they passed the blame back and forth between the Chairman and his legislative cronies and among each other. Going head to head with the Commodore this day had not gone well for any of them and it was finally sinking in. The umbrella under which these men conducted themselves was based upon the leadership and direction of their leader, William Astor. There was no house of Drew, or Gould, or Fisk. Although each was accomplished and very wealthy, they were still all part of the House of Astor. Whether in prosperity or disappointment these men had in the past and would in the future rise and fall together. It was therefore of principal import that William Astor establish an aggressive, yet conciliatory tone with his henchmen before their meeting with the Vanderbilts, "Mr. Chairman."

"Yes, Mr. Astor," responds the Chairman as the men gather in a back office waiting to conclude a settlement with the Commodore.

"Be very careful with Chauncey Depew. He's a smart Yale man."

Drew has his own strategy, "Mr. Chairman, bait the Commodore. That's how we'll make a good deal."

"Daniel, hush up," Astor quickly replies, "because of you the Chairman here and I are losing millions of dollars."

As soon as Chauncey walks into the room, the negotiation quickly begins.

First Chauncey's pleasantries, "Mr. Chairman, senators, gentlemen…"

"Where's Commodore Vanderbilt?" asks the Chairman.

Chauncey jumps right in establishing his own tone, "There's no need for his presence here tonight. Quite honestly, you're better off dealing with me because if he has his way, he'll drive the stock so high you'll all go broke."

Surrendering, "We need to get out of this deal."

This is the moment Chauncey loves, "Twice you let Mr. Drew here water the stock and then short it. Mr. Chairman, your committee debated the consolidation of the Harlem and Hudson railroads with rosy epithets, while all the time you and the other senators knew you weren't going to approve the measure. You were conspiring with Mr. Drew and were shorting the stock along with him. According to our brokers, you all began shorting when the stock was at $150 and you drove it down one hundred points. At such a cheap price, Mr. Vanderbilt would have been foolish not to start accumulating it. Yesterday, the stock hit $280 and as far as we can tell, you're all near broke."

Drew's rage is building, "You remind him who he's dealing with. We were both poor boys together and built empires for ourselves. I even gave his son Billy a job and taught him all he knows. He knew nothing before me."

"Well they've all learned a little more since, haven't they?"

"Chauncey, what does The Commodore want?" asks Astor.

"He'll let you all close out your shorts at $280 and he wants the consolidation of the Hudson and Harlem lines approved immediately."

Drew is insulted, "That's no deal."

"Perhaps you'd prefer to cover your shorts when it hits $380 or $500?"

Astor in approval nods at the Chairman, "Take the deal."

– The Breakers –

That was the first major battle between the House of Vanderbilt and the House of Astor and the Commodore had prevailed. There would be many more.

Now, a quarter century later, the fourth generation of Vanderbilts exited Mama's bedroom and adjoining sitting room to the wide eyes of family, friends, and enemies assembled in the grand hall below. As we descended the majestic staircase the applause grew and swirled around with the winds capturing the cheers from the endless thousands standing outside whom I would never know. Yet I felt as if each person wanted their hurrahs to be heard by me. As the ovation subsided, my father pulled from his coat pocket a small card containing his remarks – speech time. I knew it would be brief because Papa was a relatively shy man with a simple soul. Unlike the mess of the courtship, marriage, and eventual divorce of uncle Willie and Alva, my parents had met in church and as the eldest son and heir apparent neither of them ever had anything to prove. In some ways, society viewed him as sober and serious and the type of gentleman Mama believed I should consider. Why? Because if they are "boring" then they must be successful, unlike flamboyant men who spend their time conducting social activities rather than business affairs, or so Mama explained.

"Thank you. Thank you all for coming. Ladies and Gentlemen, my family and I are pleased that you, our close friends, are here to celebrate with us. Fortunate are we for celebrating two events tonight. The first is the long awaited re-opening of the Breakers. Let us congratulate our architect, designer, and long-time friend of the Vanderbilt family, Richard Morris Hunt, who joins us tonight with his daughter, Esther."

Everyone applauded as Esther bowed her head in my father's direction acknowledging the recognition. For the first time all night I was smiling, but it was only because I could finally see Esther. It was short lived however, as I averted my eyes when my mother turned her head in my direction.

Papa continued, "Richard, don't go building anything larger for my brother, or I'll need to hire you out again."

Everyone laughed except for Alva who stood with her new husband, Mr. Oliver Hazzard Perry Belmont, as far away as she possibly could be from Uncle Willie. On the other side of Mr. Belmont stood socialite Ward McAllister and next to him, the notorious Mrs. Astor. A little more than two decades ago, these women would never have acknowledged the others existence but today they could attend the same dinner party and engage in polite banter.

"That's not humorous." Slightly insulted, Alva whispered to her new husband, referring to the comment about her ex-husband building a larger mansion.

Not wanting to miss a word, McAllister asked Oliver, "What did Alva say?"

Oliver responded, "She didn't think that was funny."

And then the self-appointed Queen of Society, Mrs. Astor, gave her command loud enough for McAllister to hear, "shhh," but not loud enough for Alva or Oliver. She did not want to insult them by treating them disrespectfully although she certainly deemed them second fiddle.

Papa's speech continued, "To my eldest daughter, Gertrude. You are all that a father could ever ask for. As you enter society tonight at your long awaited debut, you do so with our blessings and our love."

As everyone applauded, a footman brought a tray of champagne glasses up to the landing for my parents and me while other footmen passed glasses to everyone else below us. And then my dear little brother Reggie, hidden in the small crowd, helped himself to a glass and the look on your face Victoria was golden. Anyone charged with supervising

Reggie must follow the paramount rule to ensure that he isn't swigging the hooch, yet not even an hour later, there he was with a glass, right in front of Mama. Your only hope was that it didn't get worse and maybe my parents wouldn't notice. And then, Reggie shuffled over to you and handed you his glass.

"Hold this."

You quickly responded, "I can't drink."

"It's not for you."

"And you're not allowed to drink either."

No sooner were the words out of your mouth then Reggie took a glass from another footman as Papa raised his glass, "To my daughter, Gertrude. Make the family proud and God bless to you."

Everyone raised their glass, "to Gertrude."

My eyes wandered back in Esther's direction, and then I saw him standing right behind her with his glass raised, Mr. Jim Barnes -- a friend, well perhaps a special friend. Special, because my heart adored him or such was the feeling. The question was, am I in love with him? It is so hard to comprehend. And does he love me? If he doesn't, we can never marry for only through matrimony will I experience true love. Subscribing to anything less was simply sordid, for being longed for by a man is the one thing in the world that I don't possess.

As the guests mingled about the palace casually following Papa into the dining hall, I asked you to come with me to the powder room. My duties were done and the dinner would begin regardless of my presence.

We had only been in the powder room for half a minute, enough time for you to pour me a glass of champagne while I relaxed onto the sofa, when on cue Esther walked in, sat before the mirror facing back at me, and said, "Lispenard Stewart! I can't believe you invited him."

"I did it to make Jim jealous."

"He's already jealous." Esther giggled, "That's some name. I think I'm going to start calling him, Lispy."

"You really think he's jealous?"

"You ended it with Lord Garwick. You're free to do as you please."

I rose from the sofa and walked over to her as she stared at me through the mirror.

She continued, "Lispy will dance with you tonight and you and Jim will run off to your fairy tale. The one you've always been dreaming of."

I knew what she was saying so I leaned over and put my arms around her holding her from behind. Victoria, you were the best, only there to serve and not judge or be noticed. I felt comfortable with you and so I would not hide my feelings for Esther just because you were in the room -- the ideal relationship between mistress and subject. Our most intimate moments with others or by ourselves have always been, *unter vier augen.*

To Esther my confession began, "I don't know if I should even tell you. But still there is no harm if I tell you Jim is the only man in the world I have ever allowed to do what I allowed him to do. Out of need, we were very near. He was rather restless and his foot pushed up against mine. First, I moved it away, but it happened again and this time I could not resist. I left it there. And for the rest of the evening we were thus off and on. I would have taken mine away but he always came back, not in a horrid, pushing way but-oh my God, if I was wrong, forgive me."

Esther began caressing my arms that were still wrapped around her as I kissed her neck. Her eyes half open caught every glimpse of me through the mirror, "Your mouth, Gertrude."

"Shhh. It flashed through my mind that Jim might think less of me for it, and imagine I allowed other men to do the same, but when I looked into his face, his eyes, and saw there something that made me almost shudder, I could not resist and let my foot rest against him again to show him my life was his to make or mar, just as he chose. Oh God, if it could have lasted forever."

Esther turned around to face me, "Gertrude, you someday will drive me crazy." She then slowly brought her lips to mine and whispered, "I kiss it softly at first." And when she finally kissed me on the lips, the kiss was soft and subtle at first as I gently licked her lips with my tongue. Our passion rose as she took my tongue in her mouth; excitement over took my body as I felt as if I was being lifted into the clouds as the kiss turned raw and passion over took us both "Perhaps shortly too, then for longer." She kissed me again, soft and wet "Then somehow I want all of you, entirely, and I almost care not if I hurt you."

Breathless, I don't want this to ever end, "Esther, it is one of the few thrills in life to be kissed by you and to be loved by you."

"Oh God please never let this end," as I heard myself whispering in agony with a slight tremble.

Dinner was served. Du Vain had to revise the seating chart for a fifth time on account of my invitation to Alva, her husband Oliver Belmont, and daughter Consuelo. The seats were at the head and foot of the table which were reserved for the hosts, Papa and Mama. The next most desirable places at the table were used to honor guests in order of importance in business, position in society, age, and personal preference of the lady of the house. Those thus honored were seated at the very center of the table, facilitating easy conversation with many people or to share a story. The openness of the center seats contrasted with the privacy afforded those at the head and foot.

So there they were, twenty-six of the most powerful and influential people in the world, the guardians of high society, the barons and heirs to great fortunes, and the royal houses of Vanderbilt and Astor. Each would play a role in defining the Gilded Age, mistakes made, triumphs realized, sadness, happiness, scandal, manipulation, and the *Green Eyed Monster* which would rear its head time and time again. Sitting next to Mrs. Vanderbilt at the foot of the table on her right was Alva Vanderbilt, wearing a monstrous dress from the last season with bright green ruffles on her sleeves. Someone really should have mentioned to her that the ribbon in her corset was tied askew allowing a bit more cleavage to be shown. To her left was her youngest, Gladys Vanderbilt. To Gladys' left were Gertrude, Consuelo, Esther Hunt, and her father Richard Morris Hunt, who was constantly cleaning his fork with his handkerchief in phobic bliss. Lispenard Stewart, Alfred Vanderbilt (who would not play a significant role in the family until after Papa's death), Carrie Astor Wilson (Mrs. Astor's daughter), May Wilson Goelet (wife to Ogden Goelet and sister-in-law to Carrie Astor after she married May's brother Orme), Ava Astor (wife to JJ Astor) and then the other two Vanderbilt sons, Reginald (Reggie) and Cornelius III (Neily). Continuing at the head was Cornelius Vanderbilt (my Papa), and to his left was his brother and business partner, William (Willie) Vanderbilt, followed by Chauncey Depew, Belle Wilson (one of the three Wilson sisters who in the late 1880s married a British diplomat), Ogden Goelet (New York real estate tycoon whose Newport mansion was just down the street from the Breakers), Orme Wilson (Carrie Astor's husband and brother to the three Wilson sisters), the beautifully evil Grace Wilson (the last Wilson sister, twenty-eight years old and still not married), Jim Barnes, JJ Astor (Mrs. Astor's son and heir who would become famous for having perished on the Titanic), Mrs. Astor, Ward McAllister, and finally Alva's husband, Oliver Belmont.

Before Lincoln was assassinated it was almost unheard of for northern and southern families like this to dine together in such a public way -- in Europe yes, but not in America. The Vanderbilts were northerners, the Wilsons were southerners, and the Astors while residing in New York, were southern in spirit, financial undertakings, and during the war accommodated southern slave owners in New York City's Astor Hotel. We each thought ourselves superior. One fact upon which we agreed was that the South understood that the light was shining brighter and brighter in the North – an intellectual brightness fostering human and moral evolution, though it was cold, and not just in the air. But the South was a place of pride, rich in culture, a feeling of warmth, and dominant compared to the North in economics and governance.

"Her hair sparkled and I was in my black and whites," I believe was the opening satirical piece in the Daily Herald that Edna Milli wrote after the public announcement of my debutante ball. "The light blue, almost an aqua Eilat coral, was the color of the evening. Alva was so pleased. She had dreamed of her coming out party since she could remember."

"...her greatest achievement was not having the slaves so close to the manor and providing a distraction by exposing her bosom as much as possible. Despite Abolition, without hesitation her northern friends would joyfully partake undeterred by being served by her father's mammies. She guaranteed that by making sure everyone was intoxicated. I heard a rumor that she lost it that night on top of processed but raw cotton and was caught by someone -- a jezebel it was rumored at the time. The head slave was found months later in a creek. Everybody knew Alva Erskind Smith..."

In the South it flew in the sky like a northern Christmas morning snow – the cotton was everywhere. In the years before the Civil War, *King Cotton* fueled America's emerging economy which had been struggling due to its dependence on European trade and the influential preeminent currency, the British Pound. Despite the worldwide progressive rejection of slavery, the war began not to free slaves but to prevent southern secession from the Union. Arrogantly, the Confederacy believed this was achievable as the need for cotton was equivalent to the desert's longing for water and therefore no country would dare not recognize the autonomy of the Confederate States of America.

Although the crop in the late 1850s was larger than ever, once the Civil War began and then dragged on much longer than either side expected, cotton stockpiles became low, naval blockades prevented re-supply, and as prices increased, the market found new and plentiful supplies in Egypt and India.

The war was subsidized by the Vanderbilts, Astors, and other well-to-do families buying bonds from both the North and the South, effectively financing both armies against each other. Although the North had a three to one advantage in soldiers the strategy of Confederate attrition forced the southern planters to pay enormous taxes and lose considerable wealth. While both sides issued war bonds, they both also printed money and an immense amount of it. The resulting inflation in the South was far greater than in the North and was as powerful as the gun. Yet sitting at this table in Newport during the summer of 1895 these families thrived as if the war never happened and enjoyed infinite folkloric financial and political power. Why?

The vast majority of southerners were not slave owners, not because they were ideologically opposed to the institution, but because they couldn't afford slaves. It has and will always be that while it is the rich man who starts the war it is the poor man who fights it. Those in the bourgeoisie who didn't pay or send a substitute to avoid service filled the Confederate officer corps. They were the planters, the southern Democrats who blocked the Homestead Act, and the southern tax base which, as the war dragged on and the Confederate treasury was stretched to the breaking point, compelled southern women, who had no more rights than their slaves except freedom, to demand an end to coverture. Women, of every class, entered the political arena so the poor could feed their families with inchoate welfare and the rich could resume their traditional roles as the Madame of the Plantation.

"...Alva's family had lost their money (or so she claims) not because her father was a slave owner but because he accepted Confederate currency. Unlike the Union's 'Greenback', southern currency was not legal tender and that dealt a financial blow to her family because her father never converted it to gold. Once the family, with diminished wealth, returned from Europe to New York after the war they found a society less interested in former southern planters even though her father did at least have some ethics and was known to treat most of his slaves very well..."

"...becoming an available young woman from the south was something that she had to do in order to eventually be welcomed back into New York society. Before the war such acceptance had not embraced her southern roots which made re-immersion all the more difficult. By the late 1860s Mrs. Astor and Ward McAllister were orchestrating everything about high society and her ability to marry within such circles was something impossible. Strong willed Alva however found a way by circumventing a system that she would later dominate, regret, ridicule, and ultimately change forever for every little girl and women in America. She saw first-hand how, during the war and particularly after, when the men didn't return, southern women were forced to take over the role of the 'husband' in both the home and in demanding services from the government, albeit without any rights or ability to serve in office…"

Twenty-six guests were seated in a dining room which could formally dine hundreds. It was the largest and grandest room standing stories high guarded by alabaster Roman Corinthian columns with immense carved gilt cornice that shined like diamonds in the sky. Hanging from the ceiling were Baccarat crystal chandeliers illuminating the gold gilt on all the walls. Most ironically the fresco depicts Aurora, the Roman mythological Goddess of Dawn who, seeking eternity for herself and her lover asks Jupiter for immortality for her love but tragically forgets to ask it for her. This was Alva. She wouldn't understand it for years, but Newport would provide her a sanctuary to manifest her suffrage cause and cement her role in history, a path she never would have found had she been born in the North.

Precision and perfection were the two most important attributes in the dining experience at the Breakers. Yes, the cuisine must be magnificent. Flavors must remain on the pallet. Aroma must capture imaginations. The experience of each guest must be remembered for years if the event is to be considered successful. The presentation should be artful when dressing the plate. The courses, which were twelve, must flow from one to the next in presentation, taste, and scent.

Ari Newman

The Breakers Dinner in honor of Gertrude Vanderbilt

MENU

Canapes and Crudités

Warm Oysters with shallots, cucumbers and Ossetra caviar

Soup hot or chilled

Poached Salmon with Mousseline Sauce

Filet Mignon or Saute of Chicken Lyonnaise

Lamb, Roast Duck, or Beef Sirloin
accompanied with vegetable and potato

Punch Romaine

Roast Squab and Cress

Cold Asparagus, Wild Mushroom Pastry, and Green Salad

Pate de Foie Gras

Cheese, Nuts and Dried Fruit

French Ice Cream, Waldorf Pudding and Glace, and Sec Petit Four

The meal was just a part of the extravaganza, as much effort was expended on the design of the table and its settings as went into the planning of the menu. The cutlery and China were the instruments for the art that was the feast. At the center of the canvass was the charger, which bore custom hand engraved delicate and intricate designs and was imported from Europe. To the left of the charger were the forks and to the right were the knives, while above the charger to the left was a bread plate and on the right the glasses. With twelve courses not every utensil needed for dinner was found on the table at the onset of the meal. At the start, the salad fork, dinner fork and the fish fork were placed to the left of the charger. To the right of the charger were the dinner knife, fish knife, soup spoon, and the shellfish fork. The bread knife was on top of the bread plate; from closest to the charger and moving away were the water goblet, red wine glass, white wine glass, and then the sherry glass.

Food and drinks were served, and music played softly in the background. You and Trudy stood against the wall behind the footmen. You asked her, "Who is everyone?"

"Shhh. Come here," while nudging you slightly into a hallway.

"You can't speak in there," she scolded.

"Madame du Vain told me to be certain that Neily did not speak with Ms. Grace Wilson, but I don't know who she is, and who's Neily?"

Trudy identified her at the table, "Grace Wilson. She's the blonde sitting next to Mr. Barnes across from Lispenard Stewart. He's very famous."

"Who's the handsome one sitting next to King Cornelius?"

"That's Neily. He's the eldest son. Officially he is known at Court as The Crowne Prince Cornelius Vanderbilt III," Trudy said with excitement, as her fondest passion was to gossip and was grateful whenever given the chance.

At the foot of the table, Mrs. Vanderbilt asked her niece, "Tell me Consuelo, when is the Duke arriving in Newport?"

"He's..." before Consuelo could say even a word, Alva rudely interrupted as usual.

"He's expected next month. We're having a ball in his honor and to announce the engagement."

"That sounds lovely," replied Mrs. Vanderbilt.

At the head of the table, King Cornelius commented to his brother, "You and Alva seem to have quieted down since the divorce."

"Alva had three goals in life. Divorce me, marry Consuelo to the Duke, and force Mrs. Astor to include her in her ridiculous *Four Hundred Club*."

Chauncey interjected, "Ward McAllister once informed me the name of the club was not Mrs. Astor's idea, but rather his because her ballroom in New York could only hold four hundred guests."

Uncle Willie joked with the King, "So what does Chauncey here tell McAllister -- he says, well she should just build a bigger ballroom." The three men enjoyed to laugh at Mrs. Astor's expense.

As the hour approached midnight, dinner concluded with coffee, cigars and liquors. Some of the men at the head of the table stayed and chatted and my mother was helped up by her lady's maid, Anne. My mother kissed my younger sister Gladys goodnight and then she left with Anne. Consuelo, Esther, and I remained in our seats with Trudy standing ready to serve as you took little Gladys up to bed. How she was expected to sleep that night with thousands of people screaming outside was a mystery. I also remember something that you did. Holding Gladys' hand you walked past the table, and while you didn't move your head in Neily's direction, I saw you slide your eyes in his direction and saw him stare back at you. You hinted a smile and quickly rushed off with Gladys.

The eighteen year old, shy yet proper, Consuelo was first to gossip, "What is Gracie Wilson doing here?"

I responded, "Mama invited her."

Esther couldn't believe it, "For heaven's sake why?"

"Probably so Jim Barnes and Lispy would not engage with me. It's my ball and she invites Grace, whom she doesn't even like, just to spite me."

Esther continued, "After her engagement to your…"

Consuelo interrupted, "you mean secret engagement."

"…secret engagement to your brother -- it's in poor taste that she would even accept such a social invitation."

"My mother is so evil," I thought and proudly said it out loud.

"It's not just Grace, I detest her entire family. Everyone calls them the 'Marrying Wilsons'. I just hope people in London don't refer to me as 'the marrying Vanderbilt'."

I'd been dying to ask Consuelo, "Do you love him?"

"Who?"

"The Duke."

"I don't know him. I've met him once – briefly – while we are at Blenheim Palace for a weekend. My mother spent more time with him than I did. The truth is I don't think he liked me very much."

"None of the gents who come calling fancy me. Most don't even pretend to. They see me as too tall, too skinny, goofy...The only boys I am allowed to see without supervision of a maid or my brothers."

"My mother is the same. I cannot go anywhere or see anybody without an escort." Consuelo lowered her voice and continued, "But, I have allowed Mr. Rutherford to come calling on occasion. He is considerably my senior and my mother does not suspect anything untoward."

"Really? He has a bit of a reputation." Esther exclaimed in confusion.

"Esther!"

Consuelo responded, "I've heard all the gossip and even if true, I don't care. He understands me and feels for me. He is different than all the others. He is a man. I know that he will be my first kiss – when the time is right."

I am in love with him and he is in love with me." She rose from her chair and swirled out of the room in the manner of a young girl who fell in a crush would. After Consuelo left, Esther added additional commentary, "She may be in love with him, but I cannot see him ever loving her. He is a playboy."

Esther was right. Even so, I was jealous. To kiss a man – this is something Victoria, you will likely do before me, yet you still felt for the heiress, how you wanted to be "her". You don't know what the position of a princess is. You can't imagine. She cannot do this, that, and the other simply because she is known by sight and will be talked about. You have more freedom though you own nothing, while I have everything and am in chains.

In Gladys' bedroom, a chambermaid stood at the door after placing a glass of warm milk on the bedside table while you drew down the sheets. Wearing a robe, Gladys entered from the bathroom and walked over to the bed. The chambermaid handed her the glass and Gladys slowly drank it. The room was eerily silent with the sounds of the gala creeping their way in.

When finished, Gladys handed the glass back to the chambermaid. You and the chambermaid stood behind Gladys as you removed her robe and hand it to the chambermaid. Catching you off guard, Gladys quickly fell to her knees and then the chambermaid knelt with her. You didn't know what to do so you just stood there.

Gladys began her nightly prayers, "We thank you for the forgiveness we received through Christ."

The chambermaid motioned you to kneel so Gladys wouldn't notice. Embarrassed by not being familiar with the bedtime routine, you did.

"We acknowledge our sins and imperfections," continued Gladys, "and claim the cleansing that comes through Christ. Father, we pray that you will keep us from any kind of harm and evil every moment of our lives. Send angels to watch and protect us. Amen."

"Amen."

Gladys got into bed. You approached the windows and closed the drapes against the mayhem outside the gates of the palace.

The police and the Pinkertons were keeping the crowds of thousands off the streets that surrounded the Breakers. Horse drawn carriages were turning onto Ochre Point Avenue as they entered the estate. Standing just inside the main gate, Chauncey and Simon the butler were speaking with the Newport Chief of Police. Additional police officers were running from the grounds past the three men and out the main gate to protect the arriving carriages from the crowds and the press. Everyone awaited the arrival of the first guests. Chauncey, "Simon go and inform Mrs. Vanderbilt that we are opening the front gate."

Simon ran up the path as Edna Milli shouted out a question, "We heard the Duke is actually here. Is that true, Mr. Depew?"

"No Comment."

As the flock of reporters pursued the question of the day, Chauncey appeared more and more annoyed at their never ending questions. Was he really going to reveal it even if the Duke were there? If nothing else, Chauncey's mandate was to maintain harmony between his two bosses, the brothers Vanderbilt. If it were to be revealed, Alva would be delighted with the press, Mrs. Vanderbilt would be enraged, and poor

Chauncey would have to make peace with the two women once again while not letting it distract from the business of the two brothers. Yet the questions continued about who was invited, who was wearing what, who wasn't invited and on and on. Chauncey knew that answering those questions was less harmful, and in fact gave the public what they wanted and what the newspapers wanted – gossip. As the reporters shouted questions, on cue, the unanswerable question came again from Milli and as if almost rehearsed, Chauncey covertly reached into his coat pocket, pulled out an envelope and handed it to her, "Here's a copy of tonight's press statement you asked for."

She responded, "I already saw it," but Chauncey was already gone, nowhere to be seen.

As the horse drawn carriages made their way under the Breakers iron-gate with the gold "CV" family coat of arms and proceeded onto the grounds, Edna opened the envelope and at the very bottom she saw, "not here." She had a scoop. An affirmative would have been better, but she was the first reporter with an answer and one scoop could lead to another.

The Grand Hall of the Breakers was overflowing with youthful dancing, eating, and chatting, while on the second floor galleria the Vanderbilts, the Astors, and some elder members of other royal houses were seated on chairs viewing the festivities on the first floor. The parents above watching over the children below. Standing with Trudy and Anne next to Mrs. Vanderbilt you peeked down to the hall below where in front of everyone, Lispenard Stewart danced with me turning me around and around paying the proper respect to our family and expressing support for my situation. Papa was proud even though he realized that I would never marry Lispy. My mother, however, considered it a great victory. Although he was twenty years my senior, she first entertained the idea two years earlier when it was announced in The New York Times that he was to inherit one of the great fortunes in America. Only eighteen years old, I refused to even listen until one morning, she would not let me leave the breakfast table until I had read the announcement aloud. Not surprisingly, there I was again in the Breakfast Room in front of Mama and all the morning servants reading another obituary from the estate of a family of a pre-approved gentleman:

MOURNED BY RICH AND POOR. Mrs. Lispenard Stewart buried from Grace Church. One of the wealthiest women in New York City, she was noted for her benevolence-enormous estates which date back to the time of the American Revolution, and which now pass to Mrs. Stewart's children.

I looked up at her, "it reads like the opening of the opera". "Read!" she demanded.

The funeral of Mary Rogers Rhinelander, widow of Lispenard Stewart, took place from Grace Church yesterday morning, at 10 o'clock. There was not a vacant pew in the imposing edifice, when the plain black casket was carried in on the shoulders of four stalwart employees of the Rhinelander estate. Broadway was jammed with carriages, and the sidewalk was black with people who sought admission to the church.

"I stand corrected mother. It reads like a wedding announcement." The look in her eye told me that it was the crowds that most made Lispy or any other candidate acceptable. Of course she would never have admitted it so as not to appear to be anything like Alva.

Bishop Potter met the casket at the door and led way to the altar, reading the opening sentences of the Episcopal burial service. The faint notes of a funeral march came from the organ. Following the casket were former Senator Lispenard Stewart, with Miss Serena Rhinelander, Mr. and Mrs. Frank S. Witherbee, Mr. and Mrs. William Rhinelander and the rest of the Rhinelander family...

Mama did not appreciate my editing, "every word Gertrude, every word."

Mr. and Mrs. William Rhinelander Stewart, T.J. Oakley Rhinelander, Mr. and Mrs. William Rhinelander, Mr. and Mrs. Philip Rhinelander, Mr. and Mrs. Charles E. Rhinelander, Mr. and Mrs. F.W. Rhinelander, the Misses Rhinelander, Thomas N. Rhinela, P.M. Rhinelander, Frederick W. Rhinelander, Jr. and Miss Callender.

After the casket had been placed at the front of the cathedral, which was almost buried in flowers and wreaths, the service was conducted by Bishop Potter, assisted by the Rev. Dr. Huntington, the Rev. Mr. Nelson, and Archdeacon Johnson of Staten Island and the choir.

None but the members of the family accompanied the body to the Greenwood Cemetery, where the body of Mrs. Stewart was laid to rest beside her husband in the Stewart mortuary chapel.

Among those present in Grace Church were Mr. and Mrs. Cornelius Vanderbilt and Mrs. William K. Vanderbilt, Mr. and Mrs. Fredrick Vanderbilt, Mrs. William Astor, Mr. and Mrs. John Jacob Astor, Chauncey Depew, Peter Martie, Mr. and Mrs. Bruce Price, Mayor Gilroy, Mr. and Mrs. William E. Strong..."

"I understand the point Mama. Must I read every name here? There are hundreds."

"Very well," the point was clear. Every name on this list was downstairs at my party and the message she was conveying to me in that moment was that she was mentioned first, before Alva and before Mrs. Astor and she was one of the least pretentious people I knew.

The death of Mrs. Lispenard Stewart will necessitate a redistribution of one of the largest and oldest estates in this city. She was connected with several of the local families that date back to the Revolutionary War as large landholders. William C. Rhinelander, her father, was one of the wealthiest merchants in the Unites States prior to the Civil War, and left an estate valued conservatively at $60,000,000.

On her mother's side, Mrs. Stewart was connected with the Lispenard family, which, during the days of the Revolutionary War stood on an equal footing with the Hamilton, Jay, and Fish families.

The Lispenard section of the Rhinelander estate was founded by Leonard Lispenard, who died in this city in 1790. He married Alice

Rutgers, daughter of Anthony Rutgers, who inherited one third of the extensive grant made by King George II to her father. Through purchase the remainder of the land was acquired, extending from the present Canal Street to 23rd Street, and in colonial days the Lispenard Meadows was as famous a farm as that owned by the Stuyvesants.

Leonard Lispenard was a patriot and figured prominently in the politics of the revolutionary era. He was Lispenard Stewart's great grandfather. The Rev. Thomas Barclay married Miss Rutgers, sister of Mrs. Leonard Lispenard, and brought into of the present Stewart and Rhinelander families a portion of the money and property of the Barclay estate.

When Miss Rhinelander married Lispenard Stewart, the two immense estates were united. Through judicious investment of profits in large office buildings, and because of the rapid increase in the value of land property, the Rhinelander estate is today conservatively estimated to be worth $75,000,000, from which is derived an annual income of over $3,000,000.

Following the recent death of Miss Julie Rhinelander, sister of Mrs. Stewart, her share of the estate was distributed to her remaining siblings, thereby greatly enhancing the value of Mrs. Stewart's estate. Miss Serena Rhinelander, William Rhinelander, and the family of Mrs. Lispenard Stewart are the beneficiaries of the estate. The largest portion is controlled by the three children of Mrs. Stewart: former Senator Lispenard Stewart, William Rhinelander Stewart, and Mrs. Frank S. Witherbee.

Lispenard Stewart has managed the property for several years. His office is on 14th street, near Seventh Avenue, in a two story gothic building of brick, erected in 1878, and bearing the *inscription, "Rhinelander Estate." By the division of Mrs. Stewart's share of the estate, Lispenard Stewart will become one of the wealthiest bachelors in this city.*

During her lifetime Mrs. Stewart donated immense sums of money to various charities in this city, Taking special interest in the education of indigent children, she contributed generously to the Rhinelander schools, established and managed by Miss Serena Rhinelander , and the supposition that charitable bequests will figure prominently in Mrs. Stewart's will is well founded.

Not only was Mama contemplating her own death announcement, but probably imagining how it would compare to Alva's and Mrs. Astor's. How interesting it was that in each announcement, there was no mention of the person's character, but only what they inherited and in the contents of their estates. For Mama however, I was reading this aloud so that she knew that I understood the importance of choosing the right husband. He had to come from the right family: wealthy, respected, and one of tradition. Mama's objective was simply that, an objective. I was not choosing for love, but for partnership and alliances. Perhaps the sooner I fulfill my responsibilities, the quicker I can find love, a hidden love, but never-the-less, still a love. It is one thing to fall in love. It is completely different to find love. Yet, both intertwined like a web of emotion, commitment, satisfaction, heartache, longevity…the list can go on and on, yet although a perfect match is sought, can it ever really be found? The question is how close can we get without feeling guilty but yet loyalty and fulfillment of duty. For my brother who had died at Yale, love was mythology; for me it was confusing; and for Neily it would be a fairytale that no one wanted to tell.

Oh how you felt for her? How you wanted to be her? Everything she does or says is discussed, everyone she speaks to she is suspected of going to marry, everyone loves her for what she has got, and earth is hell unless she is a fool and then it's heaven.

From the second floor, you noticed that Lispy and I were the center of attention as everyone parted like it was our first dance at our wedding, albeit a wedding that would never, and could never, happen. On the side of the hall, Neily was speaking with our neighbors, the brothers Ogden and Orme when you noticed that just as many women were focused on the three of them as were paying attention to my dance. On the other side of the hall, Grace Wilson was chatting with her sisters May and Belle, who pointed out that Neily's eyes were beamed at her.

May, "Neily is looking at you."

Belle added, "You should talk to him."

At her sister's suggestion Grace, in front of everybody, walked right past Lispy and I, almost interrupting our dance, and approached Neily. Out of the corner of your eye you observed Mrs. Vanderbilt seething at the sight of all eyes focused on Grace who was becoming the center of attention.

Grace teased Neily, "Cornelius Vanderbilt, during dinner you didn't say anything to me."

"How foolish of me. I was attending to my father and Uncle Billy."

"Well, that's as it should be. You must learn from them, as someday this will all be yours," as she moved closer to him.

"You know my mother wouldn't approve."

"I know."

Neily, totally overcome by Grace's beauty, nervously asked, "Would you care to dance?"

Neily took Grace's hand and led her to the center of the hall. Mrs. Vanderbilt had no intention of hiding her displeasure and called for Anne.

On the dance floor below, Neily whispered into Grace's ear, "my mother is watching us."

"Damn right," as she looked up at Mama and smiled.

Neily asked, "What are you doing?"

"I'm just being polite."

"You're such a liar."

If an heiress has any role at all, it is to be the center of attention. We do not engage in politics or business. Regardless of our wealth and stature; we have no voice, we have no vote. In fact, there are very few things that are required of us and even fewer rules. However, Grace was breaking that cardinal rule — never up-stage a debutante at her coming out party. Always a gentleman, Lispy quickly realized that my brother and Grace were stealing my moment, so to diminish my embarrassment he gracefully invited others to join us on the dance floor. It should have made me think that Mama was right. Lispy was not only from an appropriate family with a vast fortune but he was, and always had been, a gentleman to me. He was smart enough to understand how this dance for my benefit created jealousy within each of my perspective suitors. For this I knew Mama was grateful.

Soon Grace's eyes moved down from Mama, slid across the hall, and stared evilly at Alva and Consuelo. Realizing that both Mrs. Vanderbilts' eyes were directed with distaste at Grace, Neily cared not and said, "I see you as my brother once did."

"What?"

"Our great-grandfather would have loved you."

"The Commodore?"

"Yes. He never cared what others thought of him. I presume my mother and Alva are your adversaries and yet you want them to fear you."

Sitting on the second floor, Mama was exhausted and had watched enough, "Anne, go get Neily."

"Yes ma'am," as Anne quickly ran off.

Lispy and I graciously bowed as the music ended to everyone's cheers. It didn't take very long for Jim Barnes to approach me while I was speaking to Alva and Consuelo and he whispered something into my ear. As he did, I closed my eyes and took a deep breath. Although I couldn't understand what he was saying, I noticed Esther becoming passionately jealous.

Jim pulled back and slowly walked away.

Consuelo asked, "What did he say?"

Embarrassed I responded, "Excuse me, I'll be right back," as I followed him into the library.

Oh how you felt for her? How you wanted to be her? You don't know what the position of an heiress is. You can't imagine. The world points at her and says, "watch what she does, who she likes, who she sees, remember she is an heiress," and those who seem most amused by her are those who really remember it most vividly.

Neily and Anne made their way through the crowds to Mrs. Vanderbilt who was speaking to you, "bring some ice and a cloth to my room along with some hot tea."

"Yes, ma'am," you said.

"Neily, come with me," Mrs. Vanderbilt instructed.

They approached Mrs. Vanderbilt's sitting room and walked in between the two formal footmen standing on each side of the double doors.

"For heaven's sake Neily, what were you doing?"

"Mother, it was just a dance – one dance."

"I don't care. You are not to pursue her. Is that understood?"

As you walked in, Neily quickly dropped his quiet respectful manner, "well then why the hell did you invite her?" Anne looked shocked by Neily's tone, as you placed the ice and cloth on one table and the tea on another. Mrs. Vanderbilt walked over to Neily who was looking terrified.

"I do not answer to you."

"Yes mother. I'm sor..."

She slapped him hard across the face. Both you and Anne jumped at the loud sound. "That was for blasphemy," as Mrs. Vanderbilt turned and entered her bedroom. Anne quickly followed as the tension became so thick you could see it – red and smoky like being in a burning house during a dream and not being able to understand why you can't get out even though you are walking through the door again and again.

Neily rubbed his jaw and cheek. As soon as Mrs. Vanderbilt left the room, you ran over to the end table and wrapped the ice in the cloth. Neily, embarrassed, turned his back to you and walked to the windows. Looking outside, he saw the thousands of spectators lined around the outer gates. You walked up behind him.

"Here," as you placed the ice on his cheek.

"Thanks."

"Is there anything else I can get for you?"

Neily shook his head in the negative and so was not to embarrass him further, you turned to leave the room.

"Thanks. You are new, aren't you? What is your name?" he asked with his back still to you?

"Victoria," you replied.

"Well thank you, Victoria."

Late into the evening, people were dancing, frolicking about like adolescents, and throughout the palace people were smoking and rolling cigarettes with $100 bills. None of them noticed when Jim Barnes and I strolled through the library and opened a hidden door in the bookshelves, entering a small sitting room lit by only one candle.

For the rest of my life I shall never speak of what happened in that room behind the bookshelves. My mother wanted me to marry like Consuelo: rich, nobility, and aristocratic. Yet, that will not stop my love for Jim Barnes and I shall use all in my power to make him love me in return. And if he does, I shall marry him. I will not, however, be with Jim just to spite my mother, even though I sometimes hate her. I won't take a penny from the family even though Jim believes that his inability to support me, quietly and happily in whatever way and with whatever means, disqualifies him. Oh God, riches make more unhappiness than all the poverty in the world. Tell me, why am I rich? Oh if I could only be poor, very poor, everyone would love me for me and not for my money. What lies I speak, they still wouldn't want me at all. Oh I don't believe I will ever be happy.

We all knew why Mama invited Grace. Many thought it was because she wanted someone to dance with Lispenard Stewart to keep him away from me, but I knew the truth. It was to show Grace what she would never have. Similar to Alva, Grace was the daughter of a Southern war profiteer who manipulated Grace's siblings to marry into the richest families. May Wilson married Ogden Goelet, heir to a real estate empire second only to the Astor fortune. Belle Wilson married a British aristocrat. Brother Orme married Carrie Astor, Mrs. Astor's daughter, thereby bringing the Goelet house into the Astor Court. The newspapers continuously referred to them as the "Marrying Wilsons" so Mama understood the danger in Grace Wilson. Rumors had spread that although five years older than Neily, she had previously been engaged to my older brother, the late William Henry Vanderbilt II, whose murder just fueled more idle talk at Yale and in society. Upon his death, she quickly distanced herself, denying any romantic relationship, though she confirmed to the gossip journals that they were friends. Gossip about her was rampant in society as she always appeared to be in a relationship but would never admit it, particularly to the men courting her. Often two gentlemen would at the same time believe they were going to catch her only for both of them to be left behind and for her to have moved on, retaining all their jewels and gifts.

In the East, as the sun peeked over the Atlantic Ocean and the Cliff Walk, it illuminated the great rooms and halls in the palace. By dawn, guests were making their way out of the main entrance as you and the other members of the staff began to clear the royal residence and the outer courtyards. The footmen were still standing their posts and were joined by the Page Boys, some as young as 10 years, dressed in court livery including the quite noticeable and outdated powdered wigs. Carriages were collecting guests under the porte-cochere as they, along with the thousands who had stayed awake all night in the streets watched in awe as these young children in mass – one after the other as a great sign of wealth and power over the people – escorted the carriages under the Cornelius Vanderbilt family Coat of Arms and past the royal gates.

Across town, Captain Donnelly and Detective Grimes, three years into a case that nobody wanted solved, finally felt a glimmer of hope by finding a suspect – but no one knew it. In the weeks that followed, Edna's column in the Daily Herald would provide the exclusive headline of the summer of 1895 resulting in titanic gossip: "The Duke is Broke."

Ari Newman

Epilogue

The conclusion of Gertrude's eulogy to her brother, William Vanderbilt

I know you more now than I did
when you were here, before you left us
The pain in your eyes
The silence in your heart

Where are you now?
Shining in the rain
Flying the phoenix high
Away finally is your pain

So what to do?
No goodbyes
No more cries

Let angels fill your hollow
So tears can find escape

You deserve a second chance
So thank you for
Your fire for standing up and
Screaming out with your shout

Dramatis Personae

SECOND PERSON NARRATIVE

Victoria
18 year old maid at the Breakers who befriends and admires Gertrude

THE HOUSE OF VANDERBILT

The Commodore - Cornelius Vanderbilt
Founder

Billy - William Henry Vanderbilt
Favorite son of The Commodore

Corneel - Cornelius Jeremiah Vanderbilt
Disinherited son of The Commodore

Cornelius II - Cornelius Vanderbilt II
Billy's eldest son

Mrs. Vanderbilt - Alice Vanderbilt
Wife of Cornelius II

Neily - Cornelius Vanderbilt III
Eldest living son of Cornelius II & Mrs. Vanderbilt

Gertrude - Gertrude Vanderbilt
Protagonist and oldest daughter of Cornelius II & Mrs. Vanderbilt

Willie - William Kissam Vanderbilt
Billy's second son

Alva - Alva Vanderbilt
Billy's wife

Consuelo - Consuelo Vanderbilt
Only daughter of Billy & Alva

Chauncey Depew
President of the Vanderbilt railroad empire

THE HOUSE OF ASTOR

Mrs. Astor - Caroline Astor
Queen of high society

Jack - John Jacob Astor IV
Mrs. Astor's son

Carrie Astor
Mrs. Astor daughter who marries into the Wilson Family

Ward McAllister
The arbiter of high society and adjutant to Mrs. Astor

William Backhouse Astor, Jr.
Head of the Astor family and The Commodore's arch rival

Daniel Drew
Once mentor to The Commodore who becomes his bitter enemy

Jay Gould & Jim Frisk
Younger protégé of Daniel Drew

FEATURED CHARACTERS

Grace
The antagonist and a serial gold digger

Esther
Gertrude's taboo lover

JP Morgan
Famous banker recognized for ushering in the Industrial Revolution

Winthrop Rutherford
Most eligible bachelor in Newport

Judge Delano Calvin
Presides over the trial of The Commodore's will amongst his children

Mr. Clinton
Attorney for Billy Vanderbilt

Mr. Lord
Attorney for Corneel Vanderbilt

Judge Charles Rapallo
Reads The Commodore's last will and testament

FICTIONAL CHARACTERS

Lady X
Covert operative and contract killer

JR Perkins
Journalist, essayist, and fictional writer of *Mrs. Vanderbilt*

Edna Milli
High society newspaper reporter

Mrs. Vanderbilt

Madam DuVain
Housekeeper at the Breakers

Henry Simon
Butler at the Breakers and previous valet to Billy Vanderbilt

Trudy
Gertrude's lady's maid

Anne
Mrs. Vanderbilt's lady's maid

Inspector Cartwright
Actual name but fictional head of the Vanderbilt Pinkertons

Captain Donnelly & Detective Grimes
Responsible for protecting the Vanderbilt secrets

The Commodore

The House of Vanderbilt

William "Billy" Henry Vanderbilt

Cornelius II & Mrs. Vanderbilt

William "Willie" & Alva

Gertrude

Consuela

The House of Astor

Mrs. Astor

Carrie Astor & Orme Wilson — siblings — Grace

Cornelius Vanderbilt II & Mrs. Vanderbilt & Family

The Author

Raised in Providence, Rhode Island, Ari Newman is a film producer, lecturer, writer, amateur gourmet chef, and a community activist for which he was honored with the first Charlotte Bloomberg Award presented to him in 1993 by Mayor Michael Bloomberg. During his senior year at Boston University he produced his first feature film, *Squeeze*, which was nominated for an Independent Spirit Award and released by Miramax Films.

His films have appeared at countless international film festivals, including the Sundance Film Festival, at which *Next Stop Wonderland* was purchased for one of the largest sums ever paid for a Sundance film. In the United States he released *All My Loved Ones* starring Rupert Graves as Nicholas Winton, the stockbroker who organized the Kindertransport which saved the lives of over 600 children during World War 2 and was Slovakia's official Best Foreign Language Film submission to the 72nd Academy Awards. His most famous film is *National Lampoon's Van Wilder* considered by many to be Ryan Reynolds break out film.

Mrs. Vanderbilt is his second book. In early March 2017 he released *AMERICA FIRST A Modern Fable*, a story about a modern day civil war which became the first book to have been both written and published after the 2017 Presidential Inauguration.

Ari lives in the holy city of Jerusalem, Israel with his dog Carlos.

Made in the USA
Monee, IL
06 October 2023

08908f0a-3546-4701-9f80-2392a9da27e1R01